CHILDREN & FOOLS

THOMAS MANN

CHILDREN & FOOLS

Translated
from the German by Herman George Scheffauer

Short Story Index Reprint Series

BOOKS FOR LIBRARIES PRESS

FREEPORT, NEW YORK

First Published 1928
Reprinted 1970

INTERNATIONAL STANDARD BOOK NUMBER:
0-8369-3752-X

LIBRARY OF CONGRESS CATALOG CARD NUMBER:
71-142268

PRINTED IN THE UNITED STATES OF AMERICA

CONTENTS

DISORDER AND EARLY SORROW

DISORDER AND EARLY SORROW

THE principal dish at the midday meal had been con-
fined to vegetables; that is, to cabbage fricandeaux; it
was followed by a thin, flabby pudding, concocted
from one of the pudding-powders, tasting of almonds
and soap, which filled the shops. While Xavier, the
youthful butler, in a striped coat which he had grown
out of, in white cotton gloves and yellow sandals,
served this mixture, the Big Ones gently reminded
their father that they would have company today.

The Big Ones — that is to say, Ingrid, who was
eighteen years old and had brown eyes and was a
very charming girl, and Bert, who was fair-haired
and seventeen. Ingrid was about to graduate and was
pretty certain of passing, if only for the reason that
she was able to twist the teachers and especially the
director round her little finger and exact absolute in-
dulgence. She intended, however, to make no use of
her degree, but to force her way upon the stage, by
virtue of her agreeable smile, her equally engaging
voice, and her marked and amusing talent for parody.

Bert, for his part, was determined not to finish school at all, but to plunge into the thick of life at once, and become either a dancer, a cabaret reciter, or a waiter; the last, however, only " in Cairo " — to which end he had once made an attempt to escape the parental home, at five in the morning, an attempt that had barely been frustrated. He revealed a decided resemblance to Xavier, the butler, who was of the same age; not because he was in any way ordinary — he even bore in feature a close resemblance to his father, Professor Cornelius — but rather through some approach from another side, or at least through a kind of alternating adjustment of types, in which an extensive compromise in the matter of clothes and in general behaviour played the chief part. Both wore their thick hair very long and carelessly parted in the middle, and in consequence both had acquired the same movement of the head, whenever they tossed back an obtruding lock from their foreheads. Whenever one of them went out through the garden gate, bare-headed no matter what the weather might be, and wearing a linen Norfolk jacket belted out of sheer sportiness with a leather strap, with body bent forward and head inclined slightly upon the shoulder, and rushed off, or mounted his bicycle — Xavier indiscriminately using the bicycles of the whole family, even the

4

women's, and when he was particularly happy-go-lucky, even the professor's — then Doctor Cornelius, standing at his bedroom window, was unable, try as he might, to distinguish his son from his servant. He thought that they looked like young moujiks, one like the other. Both were passionate cigarette-smokers, even though Bert had not the means to buy as many as Xavier, who had established a record of thirty a day, smoking a brand that bore the name of a popular film-star.

The Big Ones called their parents the " Ancients " — not behind their backs, but in all affection and as a mode of address, though Cornelius was only forty-seven and his wife eight years younger. They would address father or mother as " Beloved Ancient! " or " Faithful Ancient! " The professor's parents, who led the lives of permanently astounded and intimidated old people, were called the " Arch-ancients." As to the Little Ones, Lorie and Biter, who ate in the upper nursery with " Blue Anna " — so called from the colour of her cheeks — these were accustomed to address him as their mother addressed him — that is, by his Christian name, Abel. There was something indescribably droll in the rather extravagant and ingratiating manner and tone they assumed when they called or addressed him thus, especially in

5

the sweet-chiming voice of five-year-old Eleonore, who looked exactly like Frau Cornelius in her childhood pictures, and whom the professor loved above everything.

"Ancient one," said Ingrid pleasantly, and laid her large but beautiful hand upon her father's — he was sitting at the head of the table, according to the not unnatural bourgeois tradition, while she sat to his left, opposite her mother — "good, dear ancestor, I am sure you have lost it in your subconscious. Well, it's this afternoon that we're having our little jollification, our little hop with herring salad accompaniment, and so it's up to you to keep us in countenance and not to despair — it will be all over by nine o'clock."

"Oh!" said Cornelius with long-drawn face. "All right," he added, and shook his head to show himself adjusted to the inevitable. "I merely thought — is it really today? Why, yes, it is really Thursday. How time flies! When are they coming?"

"At half past four," answered Ingrid, whose brother always permitted her to have precedence in their intercourse with the father. The guests might be expected about that time. He would hear nothing, so long as he took his nap in the second story, and from seven to eight he was sure to take his walk. He

6

might even escape by way of the terrace if he had a mind to.

" Oh! " Cornelius remarked, as much as to say: " You exaggerate."

Then Bert added, so as to have his say: " It's the only evening in the whole week on which Van doesn't have to play. He has to leave at half past six on every other day. That would be painful to all participants."

" Van " was Ivan Herzl, the popular juvenile leading man of the National Theatre. He was a great friend of Bert and Ingrid, who frequently took tea at his flat and visited him in his dressing-room. He was an artist of the new school, and adopted poses on the stage which reminded the professor of a dancer, so precious and artificial did they seem, as he stood there and yelled tragically. A professor of history is sufficiently immune to that sort of thing, but Bert had succumbed greatly to Herzl's influence and had even taken to darkening his lower eyelids, which had led to certain drastic but futile scenes with his father. Bert, with the ruthlessness and utter disregard of the young for the feelings of their elders, declared that he would not only take Herzl for his prototype in case he should decide to become a dancer, but that in the event of his becoming a waiter in Cairo he was determined to move, professionally, precisely in the same way.

7

Cornelius bowed slightly to his son, his eyebrows a trifle raised, signifying that proper diffidence and self-control suited to his generation. The pantomime was devoid of obvious irony and had a universal application. Bert might have related it to himself as well as to his friend's talent for expression.

The master of the house inquired who else was coming. Several names were mentioned, more or less known to him. There were names from the world of suburban villas, from the city, names of schoolmates of Ingrid's from the upper grade of the girls' high school — there was still some telephoning to be done. For example, there was Max to be rung up, Max Hergesell, a student of engineering, whose name Ingrid forthwith pronounced in that drawling and nasal tone which, according to her, was common to the mode of speech of all Hergesells. She proceeded with this parody in such a comic and realistic manner that her parents from sheer laughter were in danger of choking over the wretched pudding. For even in times such as these one was forced to laugh when something comic cropped up.

Then the telephone tinkled in the professor's study and the Big Ones raced over to it, for they knew that the summons was for them. Many people were forced to give up the telephone after the last increase

8

in taxes, but the Cornelius family had just managed to keep theirs, just as they had managed to keep the villa which they had built before the war, by virtue of the fact that the professor's salary was increased in proportion to the inflation of the mark. This suburban house was elegant and comfortable, even though a bit neglected, since repairs had become impossible through lack of materials, and though disfigured by iron stoves with long pipes. But all this had served as the frame for the life of the upper middle class of pre-war times, and life went on in this frame, though in a manner no longer suited to it — that is, in a needy and difficult way, in worn and turned clothes. The children had never known anything else; for them this was quite the normal order of things, they were born proletarians of the villa. The question of clothes disturbed them little. This generation had invented a costume suitable to the times, a product both of poverty and the standards of the Boy Scout; in summer it consisted chiefly of a belted jacket of linen and a pair of sandals. The bourgeois Old Ones faced greater difficulties.

The Big Ones had hung their napkins over the backs of the chairs in the adjoining room and were talking over the telephone to their friends. They who had rung up were invited guests. They were bent on accepting or declining the invitation or upon discussing this or that matter. The Big Ones negotiated with them in the jargon of their circle, a kind of slang full of bounce and queer turns of phrase, of which the Ancients seldom understood a word. The Ancients, on their part, were discussing the refreshments to be offered. The professor displayed the pride and ambition of the middle classes. He declared that there ought to be a cake or something similar, following upon the Italian salad and the black-bread sandwiches of the evening meal. But Frau Cornelius declared that this would go too far — the young people expected nothing of the sort, and the children supported her after they came back and had sat down to finish their pudding.

The housewife, whom Ingrid, though taller, resembled, was seedy and exhausted owing to the insane difficulties of the household. She ought to have gone to some health resort, but the quaking of the solid ground underfoot, the dropping-out of the bottom of things, had made this impossible for the time being. She thought of the eggs which must be bought today without fail, and began to speak of them: of the eggs at six thousand marks apiece which could be had only at a certain shop and only on this day — the shop was about fifteen minutes distant. And only a certain number of eggs were sold to each customer, so the children would have to go there at once after lunch. Danny, the son of a neighbour, would come to fetch them, and Xavier, in civilian clothes, would also accompany the young people. For this shop sold only five eggs per week to one single household, and for this reason the young folks, each assuming a different name, were to enter the shop, one after the other, in order to capture a total of twenty eggs for the Villa Cornelius. This was great sport for the participants each week, including Xavier the moujik-like, but especially for Ingrid and Bert, who were particularly bent upon mystifying and misleading their fellow beings, for the pure love of it, on every possible occasion, even when it was not a question of getting eggs.

They were fond, for example, of pretending in trams that they were somebody quite different, both by indirect means and by acting the part, and they would enter upon long, bogus conversations in a dialect which otherwise they never spoke, conversations which were quite ordinary, such as the common people carry on: the most commonplace stuff about politics and the prices of food and about persons that did not exist, so that the whole tram would listen with interest and sympathy, admiring their unlimited and ordinary glibness of tongue, though with a dark

11

suspicion that something was not quite in order here. And then they would grow still more rash and impudent and begin to tell the most horrible stories about these non-existent persons. Ingrid, assuming a high, uncertain, vulgar treble, was capable of declaring that she was a shop-girl who had an illegitimate child, a son who was a perfect monster of sadistic cruelty and who had recently tortured a cow in such an indescribable manner that no Christian soul could have looked upon it. The manner in which she would pronounce the word "tortured" in her chirping voice would bring Bert to the verge of exploding, but he would manage to control himself and manifest a kind of ghastly interest. And then he and the unfortunate shop-girl would begin a long and dreadful talk, at once stupid and wicked, as to the nature of such pathological cruelty, until some old gentleman, sitting diagonally opposite, with his tram-ticket carefully folded and tucked between his forefinger and his seal-ring, would discover that the limit had been reached and object publicly to such young people's discussing themes of this sort in such detail. Ingrid would thereupon pretend that she was about to dissolve into tears, and Bert would apparently be seized by a deadly rage at the old gentleman, which he would be able to suppress only by the greatest efforts, though

12

not for any length of time. He would clench his fists and gnash his teeth, and a trembling would go through his entire body, so that the old gentleman, who had meant well enough (the thing really happened) thought it best to leave the tram hurriedly at the next stop.

Such were the amusements of the Big Ones. The telephone played a prominent part. They rang up all sorts of persons, opera singers, high officials, and princes of the church, introduced themselves as saleswomen or as Count and Countess Mannsteufel, and were very difficult to persuade that they had got the wrong number. On one occasion they emptied the tray of visiting-cards and distributed the cards higgledy-piggledy — but not without a certain feeling for the bewildering half-likelihood of things — in the letter-boxes of the quarter, whence proceeded great perturbation, since suddenly God knows who appeared to have visited Heaven knows whom.

Xavier, who had taken off his white cotton serving-gloves, so that the yellow chain-ring which he wore upon his left hand was seen, now entered to clear the table, tossing his hair; and while the professor drank up his "thin beer" at eight thousand marks a bottle, and lighted a cigarette, the Little Ones could be heard scampering downstairs and along the hall. They were

13

coming as usual to greet their parents after lunch, storming the dining-room, battling with the door, to the knob of which they clung both together with their little hands, and then came in stamping and stumbling with hurrying, awkward little legs across the carpet, their feet covered with little red slippers of felt, over which their stockings had crept down in many folds and wrinkles. Each, shouting, explaining, and chattering, steered towards his accustomed goal. Biter headed for his mother and climbed into her lap to tell her how much he had eaten and as if in testimony thereof to show her his distended stomach, while Lorie went to her " Abel " — who was so very much her own because she was so very much his own, and because she sensed the heart-felt and, like all deep emotions, somewhat melancholy tenderness with which he embraced her little feminine person and drank it in smilingly, and also the love with which he regarded her and kissed her exquisitely formed little hands, or her temples, upon which the delicate blue veins made such a tender and moving pattern.

The children revealed the strong yet indecisive similarity of a brother and sister, a likeness which was augmented by similar clothing and arrangement of the hair; and yet again, in the sense of male and female, they differed conspicuously from each other.

14

They were a little Adam and a little Eve, that was
clearly evident — evidenced especially on Biter's
side by a certain consciousness and self-reliance; he
was more set in his figure, stockier, stronger, and em-
phasized his four-year-old manly dignity in carriage,
mien, and manner of speaking by letting his arms de-
pend athletically from his slightly raised shoulders
like a young American, or, when speaking, by drawing down the corners of his mouth and attempting to
give his voice a deep, cheery ring. As a matter of fact,
all this dignity and manliness was a show rather than
an essential part of his nature, for he had been born
and nursed in times of frantic upset, and his nervous
system was very sensitive and unstable; he suffered
severely from the petty annoyances of life, was disposed to be irascible, and often gave way to fits of
fury, to embittered and despairing floods of tears over
every trifle — and was for this very reason the special pet of his mother. He had a longish little nose,
a small mouth, and round eyes of chestnut-brown,
which were inclined to squint a little and foretold the
early wearing of a pair of corrective spectacles. The
nose and the mouth were those of his father, as had become very evident since the professor had shaved off
his pointed beard. (He had clung to this pointed beard
as long as possible, but even an historical individual

15

must finally make concessions to the customs of the present.) Cornelius held his little daughter upon his knee, his little Eleonore, his little Eve — so much more gracile, so much sweeter in expression than the boy — and, holding his cigarette far away from her, let her finger his spectacles with her delicate little hands, for the lenses, divided into sectors for reading and for vision at a distance, were objects of daily curiosity to her.

At heart he had a feeling that the predilection of his wife was a more magnanimous choice than his own, and that Biter's difficult masculinity might weigh more in the scheme of things than the harmonious winsomeness of his little girl. But the heart, he reflected, will suffer no dictate, and his heart, after all, had belonged to the little girl ever since she came, ever since he saw her for the first time. And whenever he held her in his arms, that first time came back to him. He remembered the bright room in the Woman's Hospital in which little Lorie first saw the light — twelve years lay between her coming and that of her elder brother and sister. He had entered the room, and almost at the very moment in which, attended by the smiles of the mother, he had carefully drawn back the curtain of the little canopied doll's bed that stood beside the larger one, and had become conscious of the tiny mar-

16

vel which lay there amidst the cushions, so beautifully formed and surrounded, as it were, by a clarity of sweetness and harmonious proportion, with hands which were even then, though on a smaller scale, as beautiful as now, with wide-open eyes which were even then of a heavenly blue and reflected the shining day — at that very moment he had felt his heart seized and made captive. It was love at first sight and for ever, a feeling which, unknown, unexpected, and unhoped for — so far as his consciousness was concerned — utterly possessed him and which he at once comprehended, joyfully and with surprise, as being something that would be valid for life.

Doctor Cornelius, moreover, knew that, properly considered, he might have been mistaken as to the utter unexpectedness, the unhoped-for-ness, of this feeling, as well as its complete arbitrariness. He knew at heart that it could not have overcome him by mere chance and become a part of his life, but that somehow, even though unconsciously, he must have been prepared for it, or, more correctly, been ready for it; that something within him was ready to engender it in his heart at the given moment, and that this something, strange to say, was his character as a professor of history. Doctor Cornelius was not wont to say this — he was merely sometimes aware of it, and then he

17

indulged in a mysterious smile. He knew that professors of history do not like history, in so far as it is history that happens, but only as history that has happened; that they hate the upheavals of the present, because they are lawless, disconnected, and impudent — in one word, " unhistorical " — and that their heart is with the coherent, proper, and historical past. And when the professor took his walk along the river before dinner, he was wont to confess to himself that the spirit of the timeless and the eternal lay over the past, and that this spirit was much more congenial to the nerves of a professor of history than all the insolence of the present. The past is perpetuated — that is to say, it is dead; and death is the source of all seemliness and permanent significance. The doctor was secretly convinced of this, when he went walking alone in the dark. It was his preservative instinct, his sense for the " eternal," which caused him to save himself from the cynical asperities of the times by taking refuge in his love for this little daughter of his. For paternal love and a child at the breast of a mother — these are timeless and eternal and therefore beautiful and holy. And yet, when he pondered in the dark, Cornelius understood that there was something that was not quite right and good in this love of his — he conceded it theoretically for the sake of knowledge. This

18

love of his, judging by its origin, was fettered to a certain tendency; there was hostility in it, opposition to history in the making, and inclination in favour of history that was made — that is to say, death. Extraordinary enough, to be sure, yet true, true to some degree. His passion for this sweet little piece of life and progeny was in some way connected with death; it was a passion that remained faithful to him, and arraigned itself against life, and this, in a certain sense, was not well, not as it should be, although it would naturally have been the maddest kind of asceticism to stifle the purest and loveliest emotion of his heart because of such an occasional and purely scientific insight into things.

He held his little daughter upon his knees, and her thin, rosy little legs hung down beside his own. He spoke to her, his eyebrows raised, in a tone of tender and comic reverence, and listened with rapture to the sweet, piping voice in which she answered him, calling him " Abel." He exchanged eloquent glances with the mother, who was attending to her Biter and gently advising him to be sensible and well-behaved, for, being unduly vexed by life's little ironies, he had had another attack of temper today and had acted like a howling dervish. From time to time Cornelius also cast a half-suspicious glance towards the Big Ones, for

19

he felt it not impossible that they were familiar with certain learned analyses in connexion with his evening walks. But if this was so, they did not betray it. They stood behind their chairs and leaned their arms upon the backs, regarding this parental idyll benevolently, if not without a trace of irony.

Both children wore thick, embroidered modern " art " dresses of a brick-red colour, which had in their time been worn by Bert and Ingrid, and which were both alike, with the single exception that Biter's revealed a pair of short tiny trousers under the skirt. Both wore their hair bobbed in precisely the same manner. Biter's hair was irregularly blond, and still in the process of slowly darkening. It was awkward, stubborn hair, very bristly, and resembled a funny little ill-fitting wig. Lorie's, on the contrary, was chestnut-brown, silky, and glossy, and as agreeable as her entire little person. It covered her ears, which, as they all knew, were not alike in size, the one being of proper proportions, the other somewhat out of scale, decidedly too large. Her father at times laid bare these ears, and would then express his amazement in loud exclamations, as though he had never before observed this slight defect, something which at once amused and shamed Lorie. Her golden-brown eyes were wide apart, and full of a sweet, soft shimmer

20

and the clearest and most lovable expression. Her eye-brows were fair. Her nose was still pudgy, with nostrils slightly thick, so that the openings were almost round; her little mouth was wide and very expressive, with a finely carved and mobile upper lip. When she laughed and showed her pearly but widely separated little teeth (she had lost only one so far — her father had forced the wobbly thing out with his handkerchief, which had caused her to grow very pale and to tremble), then dimples came into her cheeks, which in spite of their childish softness were given their somewhat hollow form by the slight projection of the lower half of her face. On one cheek, close to the soft fall of her hair, she had a downy mole.

On the whole, she was by no means satisfied with her appearance — a sign that it was a matter of concern to her. Her face, she sadly concluded, must, unfortunately, be regarded as plain; her " figger," on the contrary, was quite nice. She loved choice, refined little expressions and used them in strings, such as " perhaps, to be sure, in the end." Biter's self-critical worries were more concerned with moral factors. He inclined to abject contrition, and considered himself on account of his fits of rage a great sinner who would never go to heaven. Arguments were futile, such as God's having a great deal of consideration and not

21

being always disposed to even up the odds. Biter would merely shake his head and that ill-fitting wig of his in a kind of obstinate melancholy, and declare that his chances of attaining heavenly felicity were absolutely nil. Whenever he caught cold, he appeared to be entirely full of phlegm, and one had only to touch him to make him wheeze and rattle; he was also disposed to have the highest possible fever at once, so that he panted. The nurse-maid Anna was on such occasions inclined to the most sombre predictions in respect to his constitution and vouchsafed the opinion that a boy with such " uncommonly thick blood " might succumb to apoplexy at any moment. One day she thought that this terrible moment had really arrived. Biter, in punishment for a berserker-like fit of fury, had been put into a corner with his face to the wall, and had, upon chance inspection, revealed this face blue all over, much bluer than Anna's own. She had drummed the whole house together, announcing loudly that the excessive thickness of the boy's blood had brought about his last hour. The wicked Biter suddenly found himself, to his just amazement, overwhelmed with the tenderest solicitude, until it became clear that the blueness of his features was not due to congestion, but to the calcimined wall of the nursery, which had transferred some of its indigo to his tear-stained face.

22

Anna the nurse-maid had also come in now and stood with folded hands near the doorway — a vision in a white apron, with oily hair, fishy eyes, and an expression revealing the rigorous dignity of her limitations. " The children," she declared, proud of her care and training, " are deciphering themselves wonderfully." She had recently had seventeen ragged stumps removed from her jaws, and an even set of yellow artificial teeth with dark-red gutta-percha gums fitted, which now beautified her stolid peasant face. Her mind was beset by the remarkable hallucination that this set of teeth was the talk of the whole neighbourhood, that the very sparrows on the roof had nothing else to chatter about. " There has been a lot of idle talk," she said, in a severe and mysterious manner, " because, as you know, I have had a set of teeth made." She had a constant inclination to the use of dark and murky speech, which others were incapable of penetrating, as, for example, concerning a certain Dr. Bleifuss, who was known to every child, " and there are others living in that house," she said, " who pretend to be him! " One was forced to be lenient and ignore her utterances. She taught the children lovely verses, as, for example:

> " Railway-train, railway-train,
> Going or still,
> Freight-train or passenger,
> Whistle it will."

Or that weekly bill of fare, so full of privations and yet so fitting to the times, which runs:

> " Monday morn the week begins.
> Tuesday minds us of our sins.
> Wednesday is the middle of it.
> Thursday brings us little profit.
> Friday noon we eat the fish,
> Saturday dance round the dish.
> Sunday there's a lovely roast,
> And a salad too we boast."

There was also a quatrain of incomprehensible and insoluble romanticism:

> " Throw wide the door, throw wide the door,
> Let the big carriage roll.
> Who sits within it all in state?
> A lord with hair of gold! "

And finally there was an outrageously vivacious ballad of Little Marie, who sat on a stone, a stone, a stone, and combed her likewise golden hair, golden hair, golden hair. And another of Rudolf, who drew a knife, drew a knife, drew a knife out, and who came to a fearful end.

Lorie was able to say and sing all this with her mobile little mouth and her sweet voice — much better than Biter. She was in fact able to do all things better than he, for which he honestly admired her and subordinated himself to her, apart from attacks of rebellion and of choleric combativeness. She often instructed him in a pedagogic sense, explained to him the birds in the picture-book, made them clear to him by vivid names: the cloud-eater, the hail-eater, the raven-eater. She made him repeat these after her. She also gave him pointers about medicine, and illness, such as inflammation of the lungs, inflammation of the blood, " inflammation of the air." When he did not pay attention or was unable to repeat the words after her, she put him in a corner. Once she even added a box on the ears, but she was so ashamed of this that she went and stood in the corner herself for a long time.

Without a doubt, the children got on splendidly together; they were one heart and one soul. They experienced all things, all adventures, in common. They would come in from a walk and relate in great excitement and as with one voice that they had seen " two moo-moos and a veal " on the country road. With the servants below stairs, with Xavier and with the

Hinterhöfers, two once prosperous middle-class sisters who undertook " *au pair*," as the expression goes, to fulfil the offices of cook and chamber-maid, they were on a most familiar footing — at least they seemed to feel at times a certain likeness between the relation of these subordinates to their parents and their own. Whenever they were scolded, they would go into the kitchen and say: " The master and mistress are real mad! " Nevertheless there was always much more fun playing with those " higher up," and especially with " Abel," when he was not obliged to read or write. He always thought of far more wonderful things to do than Xavier or the ladies. They would play at being " four gentlemen," and go walking. " Abel " would then crook his knees until he was the same height as themselves, and set forth on the walk hand in hand with them, a sport of which they never had enough. They would have been content to go promenading with the diminished " Abel," five gentlemen all in all, the whole day long, round and round the dining-room.

There was furthermore the extremely exciting cushion game. This consisted of one of the children, usually Lorie, sitting down in a chair at the dining-table, apparently unobserved by " Abel," and still as a mouse awaiting his coming. Gazing idly about him, amid exclamations which clearly and loudly attested his faith in the comfort of his chair, he would draw near and seat himself on Lorie. " Hello! " he would say, " what's this? " And then he would squirm back and forth, without hearing the suppressed tittering behind him. " Somebody has put a cushion on my chair! My! what a hard, crooked, awkward cushion it is! How do they expect me to sit comfortably on it? " And then he would begin to slide harder than ever on the strange and awkward cushion, and finally reach behind him right into the midst of all that ecstatic tittering and giggling, until he turned round, and a great climax of discovery and recognition would conclude the drama. This game, too, would lose nothing of its fascinating tension though repeated a hundred times.

Today there was no time for such pleasures. The restlessness of the impending party of the Big Ones hung in the air, and there was also the purchasing to be done beforehand, each enacting his role. Lorie had just finished reciting " Railway-train, railway-train," and Doctor Cornelius, to her great chagrin, had just discovered that her ears were of different sizes, when Danny, the neighbour's son, came in to fetch Bert and Ingrid. Xavier had also exchanged his striped livery for an ordinary jacket, which immediately gave him a somewhat bounderish, even though smart and agreeable, air. The Little Ones thereupon ascended to the upper realm, under the wing of Anna. The professor withdrew into his study to read, as was his custom after meals, while his wife, thinking of the anchovy sandwiches and the Italian salad, began to prepare these for guests who would be coming to the dance. She was also obliged to run into town on her wheel before the young people arrived, in order to convert a sum of money which she feared might be suddenly devalued, into table supplies.

Cornelius was reading, leaning far back in his armchair. With his cigar poised between index and middle finger, he was reading in Macaulay about the origin of the English national debt at the close of the seventeenth century, after which he took up a French author and read about the growing indebtedness of Spain towards the close of the sixteenth century — both subjects of his lecture the following morning. He was going to compare England's surprising commercial prosperity of that time with the fatal results which the national indebtedness had produced in Spain a century before, and analyse the ethical and psychological results of the difference. This would give him an opportunity to proceed from the England of William III, the period actually in question, to the age of Philip II and the Counter-Reformation, which was his particular hobby, and concerning which he

28

had written a book — a much-quoted work, to which he owed his professorship. While his cigar was growing short and somewhat acrid, he revolved in his mind a few sentences tinged with gentle melancholy, intending to visit them upon his students the following morning. These sentences referred to the practically hopeless battle of this slow King Philip against the new era, against the course of history, and the imperially disintegrating force in the Germanic ideal of individual liberty — they dealt with the battle, condemned by life and therefore accursed of God, between obdurate aristocracy and the powers of progress and of change. He found the sentences good and kept on filing away at them, then put the books back into the bookcase, and went up to his bedroom, in order to give a kind of cæsural pause to his workday — that treasured hour with closed blinds and closed eyes which had become a necessity to him, and which, as he remembered after his scholarly digression, was to be subjected today to the inroads of festal domestic disquiet. He smiled at the slight perturbation of nerves which this memory aroused in him. The draft of his sentences about Philip clad in black silk mingled itself in his mind with thoughts of the dance that was to be given by his children, and then for five minutes or so he fell asleep.

29

While he lay there and rested, he heard the door-bell ring repeatedly, heard the garden gate fall to, and each time felt the sting of a slight excitement, of expectation and oppression at the thought that the young people were arriving and were beginning to fill the lower hall. These tiny shocks caused him to smile, and yet he knew that these smiles were essentially only the expression of a nervousness, which was natu-rally compact also of a certain exhilaration, for who would not feel joy at the prospect of a merry-making? At half past four (it was already evening) he arose and freshened himself up at the wash-stand. The wash-bowl had been cracked for more than a year. It was a hanging basin, made to tip, but the pivot was out at one side and could not be repaired because a workman could not be had, nor could it be replaced, because no shop could supply another. It was there-fore suspended provisionally over the outlet on the edges of the marble slab, and could be emptied only by being lifted with both hands and poured out. Scarcely a day passed but Cornelius shook his head over this wash-bowl, as he again did now. He then finished tidying himself — very carefully — pol-ished his glasses under the ceiling light until they were clear and transparent, and started down to the dining-room.

As he descended the stairs, he heard the voices below, already a medley, and the gramophone already set going. His features assumed a polite and conciliatory company expression. He decided to say: " Please don't disturb yourselves! " and then to go right into the dining-room and have his tea. This formula appeared to him the proper one in the circumstances, serene and considerate in its external effect, as well as a good defence for himself.

The hall was brightly illuminated; all the electric bulbs of the electrolier were aflame, all save one that was burnt out. Cornelius stood still on one of the lower steps of the stairs and surveyed the hall. It made a pretty picture in the mellow light, with the copy of an old master over the brick fireplace, with the panelling, which was of soft wood, and with the red carpet, on which the guests were standing about, tea-cup in hand, chatting and eating small sandwiches spread with anchovy paste. The atmosphere was quite festive, a slight aura of dresses, hair, and warm presences pervaded the hall — something that was characteristic and charged with memories. The door of the cloak-room stood open, for new guests were still arriving.

Such social scenes dazzle at first; the professor received only a general impression. He had not noticed that Ingrid, in a dark silk dress with a white accordion-

31

pleated cape-collar and bare arms, was standing close in front of him, surrounded by her friends, at the bottom of the steps. She nodded to him and smiled, showing her fine teeth.

" Have you had a good rest? " she asked softly, as though between themselves. And then, after he had recognized her with a surprise that seemed unjustified, she introduced him to her friends.

" May I introduce Herr Zuber? " she asked. " And this is Fräulein Plaichinger."

Herr Zuber was not much to look at; the Plaichinger girl, on the other hand, was a valkyrie, blonde, full-bosomed, and loosely dressed, with a pug-nose and the high treble of buxom femininity, as became evident when she replied to the professor's polite greeting.

" You are surely most welcome," he said. " It is awfully nice of you to give us this pleasure. You are a class-mate of Ingrid's? "

Herr Zuber was a member of Ingrid's golf club. He was preparing for a business career, and was employed in the office of his uncle's brewery. The professor made a few jokes about the " thin beer," in which he pretended to overrate to an excessive degree the influence of young Zuber upon the quality of this beer.

" Now, don't let yourselves be disturbed in any

32

way," he remarked, and was about to cross over to the dining-room.

"And here comes Max!" said Ingrid. "Say, old man, what do you mean, barging in here so late, after the dance is on?"

The "*du*" or familiar "thou" form of address was common to all these young people, and their forms of intercourse were strange to their elders — there was little trace of strict breeding, gallantry, or drawing-room manners.

A young fellow with an exposure of white shirt-front and a small dress tie advanced from the cloak-room towards the staircase and saluted them. He was dark, but with rosy, smooth-shaven cheeks and with slight side-burns close to his ears, a really handsome youth, not ridiculously nor gaudily pretty, like a gipsy violinist, but masculinely handsome in a very agreeable, well-bred, winning manner, with friendly black eyes. His dinner-jacket still sat a bit awkwardly upon him.

"Now, now, don't scold me, Cornelia," he said, using the feminine form of her family name. "It was that confounded lecture." Ingrid presented him to her father: Herr Hergesell.

So this was Herr Hergesell. He thanked the master of the house in a courteous manner for having invited

33

him, and they shook hands. " I'm a bit late," he said, jovially; " it happened that just today I had a lecture until four o'clock, and then, of course, I had to rush home and change my clothes." Then he spoke of his pumps, which had just given him great trouble in the cloak-room.

" I brought them along in a bag," he said. " I couldn't expect to go tramping all over your carpets here in my street shoes. But I stupidly forgot to bring along a shoe-horn, and, by Jove, I couldn't get into them at all — imagine the stupid fix! I've never had such tight pumps in my life. The sizes are all different now, there's no depending on them, and then the stuff they use nowadays! — why, it isn't leather at all, it's hard as cast iron! I've mashed my whole finger." He showed his reddened forefinger confidentially, and referred to the episode again as a " fix," and a most disgusting one. He spoke in precisely the way Ingrid had imitated — in a very nasal manner, with a peculiar drawl, obviously without affectation, because it was the habit of all Hergesells to talk that way.

Doctor Cornelius expressed regret that there had been no shoe-horn in the cloak-room and manifested due sympathy for the forefinger. " Now, you mustn't let me disturb you in the slightest," he said; " *auf wiedersehen!*" and he crossed the hall to the dining-room.

Here too there were guests. The dining-table had been drawn out full length, and tea was being served at it. But the professor went straight to his own little nook, which was tapestried with embroidery and lighted by its own little ceiling light, where stood the small round table at which he was accustomed to drink his tea. He found his wife there, engaged in conversation with Bert and two other young gentlemen. One of them was Herzl; Cornelius recognized and greeted him. The other was called Möller — a type of the "*Wandervogel*," who apparently neither possessed nor cared to possess a suit of ordinary party clothes, bourgeois clothes (the concept really meant very little any more). He was a young fellow who was evidently not at all ambitious to play the " gentleman " (another concept which had become vitiated). He wore a linen blouse with a belt and knickers, a thick mane of hair, and horn-rimmed spectacles. His neck was long and thin. He was engaged in a bank, as the professor discovered, but in addition to this he was also active as a kind of artistic folk-lorist, a collector and singer of folk-ballads from all zones and tongues. He had brought along his guitar, by special request. It was still hanging in its oilcloth cover in the cloak-room.

Herzl, the actor, was small and slight, but he had a strong black beard, as was evident from too heavy powdering after his shave. His eyes were over-large, glowing, and melancholy. In addition to the large quantities of powder he had used, he had apparently applied also a bit of rouge — the faint carmine upon his cheek-bones was obviously of cosmetic origin. " How remarkable! " thought the professor; one would imagine that he would cling to either one thing or the other — either to his melancholy or to his rouge. Taken together they formed a psychological contradiction. Why should a misanthrope rouge himself? But here, no doubt, was the peculiar, alien form of the artistic nature, which rendered this contradiction possible, or even consisted of it. Well, it was interesting and no real reason for his not being quite hearty with him. It was a legitimate thing, possibly a primitive thing. — " Will you have lemon in your tea, *Herr Hofschauspieler* — Herr Court Actor? "

Court actors, of course, were a thing of the past, but Herzl was fond of the title, despite the fact that he was a revolutionary artist. And that was another contradiction which was part of his spiritual equipment. The professor had rightly conjectured that this contradiction existed, and hence flattered him, as a kind of reparation for the secret repugnance he had felt upon becoming aware of the light shade of rouge on Herzl's cheeks.

" My most devoted thanks, my dear Herr Professor," said Herzl, so hurriedly that he was saved from tangling his tongue only by means of his superb elocutionary technique. His attitude towards his hosts, and especially towards the master of the house, was inspired by the greatest degree of respect; it was in fact almost excessively, even subserviently, polite. It was as though he felt a certain sense of guilt because of the rouge, which some inner compulsion had forced him to apply, but of which he disapproved, for the same reasons perhaps as the professor himself, and sought to conciliate an unrouged world by the greatest modesty he could muster.

Conversation went on, while tea was being drunk, passing from Möller's folk-songs, from Spanish and Basque folk-songs, to the new production of Schiller's *Don Carlos* at the National Theatre, a production in which Herzl was to play the title-role. He began to talk of his interpretation of Don Carlos. " I hope," he said, " that my Don Carlos will be a perfect unity, an organic whole." There was also critical talk of the cast, of the values of the scenery, of the atmosphere and the *milieu;* and almost before he was aware, the professor saw himself steered into his favourite channel, the

37

Spain of the Counter-Reformation, which affected him rather painfully. He was quite innocent; he had done nothing to give the conversation this turn. He was seized by the fear that it might look as though he had sought an opportunity to lecture, began to wonder, and then relapsed into silence. He was glad when the Little Ones, Lorie and Biter, came to the table. They were dressed in blue velvet, their Sunday apparel, and were bent on participating in their own fashion in the fun of the Big Ones until bedtime. They said good-evening to the strangers shyly, making big eyes the while, and were then called upon to tell their names and their ages. Herr Möller merely regarded them earnestly, but Herzl, the actor, was entirely carried away by them, enchanted and ecstatic. He almost blessed them, raised his eyes to heaven, and folded his hands over his mouth. There was no doubt that he was sincere in this, but his being accustomed to theatrical conditions and effects caused his words and actions to appear frightfully false. And, moreover, it was as though his devotion to the children was also to serve to reconcile one to the rouge upon his cheek-bones.

The tea-table was now deserted by the guests, dancing had begun in the hall, the Little Ones ran to be part of it, and the professor decided to retreat to his own room. " I hope you'll have a good time," he said, as he shook hands with young Möller and Herzl, both of whom had sprung to their feet. And then he walked over to his study, to his own fenced-in empire. Here he let down the outer shutters, turned on the writing-table lamp, and sat down to work.

It was work which in an emergency might easily have been done even in an unquiet environment — a few letters, a few quotations. Cornelius, of course, was *distrait*. He was still haunted by minor impressions, the inelastic pumps of young Hergesell, the high falsetto emanating from the robust body of Fräulein Plaichinger. His thoughts also reverted to Möller's collection of Basque songs, while he wrote, or, leaning back in his chair, stared at emptiness, and they hovered about Herzl's humility and exaggerations, " his " Carlos, and the court of King Philip. Conversations, he mused, were strange, mysterious things. They were plastic, and even when undirected, pursued some secret, dominating interest. He seemed to have noticed this frequently. In the intervals he listened to the by no means noisy sounds of the house-dance outside. There was talk to be heard, but not a trace of the shuffling sounds of the dance. But then, they no longer circled and shuffled, they merely walked round the carpet in a peculiar manner, nor were they disturbed by the folds of the carpet. They

39

took hold of one another in a fashion to which he had not been accustomed in his time, and did this to the tunes of a gramophone, tunes which particularly engaged his attention — these peculiar melodies of the New World, the instrumentation of which was jazzy, with all kinds of percussion pieces, which the talking-machine reproduced excellently. There was also the smacking clack of the castanets, but these affected him as merely a part of the jazz noises and not at all as Spanish. No, Spanish they were not. And then he was once more in the midst of his professional thoughts.

After the lapse of half an hour he suddenly remembered that it would be no more than hospitable to contribute a box of cigarettes to the festivities. It would not be proper, he reflected, to have the young people smoke their own cigarettes — though they would think nothing of it. And so he went into the empty dining-room and took a packet from his supplies in a little wall-cupboard. He did not select precisely the best, at least not those which he himself preferred to smoke, but a rather long, thin format, which he was glad to get rid of by this opportunity, for, after all, they were young people. He went into the hall, lifted the box on high with a smile, and placed it open upon the mantel-piece; then, after a brief, swift survey, turned to go back to his room.

Just then came an interval in the dance — the gramophone was silent. The young folk sat and stood about the walls of the hall and chatted, some of them grouped around the heraldic table near the windows, others on chairs in front of the fireplace. Some were perched upon the steps of the built-in staircase, sitting on the rather threadbare plush stair-carpet, and arranged amphitheatrically. Max Hergesell, for example, sat there with the buxom, high-voiced Plaichinger girl, who was looking directly into his face, while he, in a half-reclining posture and with one elbow supported on the step immediately behind him, gesticulated with the other hand while speaking. The main floor-space of the biggish room was empty; only in the centre, directly under the electrolier, the two Little Ones were visible in their blue dresses, awkwardly embracing, gravely and slowly turning about each other. Cornelius, in passing, bent over and, with a gentle word, stroked their hair. But they would not allow themselves to be disturbed in their solemn and infantile undertaking. Looking back from the door of his study, he observed that young Hergesell, probably because he had noticed the professor, had heaved himself up from the step with his elbow, and had come down to take Lorie out of the little arms of her brother, and to dance with her himself in a droll way,

41

without music. His actions were almost like those of Cornelius himself when he went walking with "four gentlemen." He bent his knees out, and sought to hold her like a grown person, and then made a few shimmy-steps with bashful little Lorie. All those who had observed it were much amused. It was the signal for once more turning on the gramophone and resuming the dance. The professor, with the door-knob in his hand, regarded the scene for a moment, nodding and shrugging his shoulders whimsically, and then entered his room. For some minutes longer his features mechanically retained the smile he had brought in from outside.

He once more began turning over papers under the light of his table-lamp, began to write, and then concluded a few trifling matters. After a time he became aware that the company was leaving the hall and moving over to his wife's drawing-room, which was directly connected with his study as well as with the hall. Voices were now heard here and the experimental strumming of a guitar. Young Möller was going to sing, was, in fact, already singing. The young bank-clerk was singing a song in an alien language, with a powerful bass voice, and accompanying it with chords from his guitar. The song, which was received with great applause, was possibly Swedish, although the professor, who had listened until the close, was unable to distinguish this with any degree of certainty. For the purpose of deadening sound, a thick curtain hung over the door that led to the drawing-room. Then a new song began and Cornelius went cautiously over to the drawing-room.

Half-darkness prevailed there. Only the draped standing-lamp was lit and Möller sat close to it with crossed legs on a cushion of the antique chest; his thumb wandered among the strings. There was no order in the arrangement of his audience; it bore the impress of chance and help-yourself-as-best-you-may, for there were not enough chairs to go round. Some were standing, though many, among them some of the young ladies, were simply sitting on the floor, on the carpet, clasping their knees with their arms, or even stretching out their legs at full length. Hergesell, for example, was sitting on the floor in spite of his dinner-jacket, close to the legs of the grand piano, and beside him crouched Fräulein Plaichinger. The Little Ones were also there: Frau Cornelius was ensconced in her arm-chair facing the singer and was holding both of the children on her lap. Biter, the barbarian, began to talk aloud right in the middle of the song, so that it was necessary to intimidate him by " sss-sshes " and by shaking a finger at him. Lorie would never have

43

been guilty of a thing like that; she sat daintily and quietly on her mother's lap. The professor sought to catch her eye, in order to wave to her in secret; but she did not see him, even though she was not apparently paying any attention to the singer. Her eyes went deeper.

Möller sang the " *Joli tambour* " :

" *Sire, mon roi, donnez-moi votre fille —* "

They were all charmed. " How good! " Hergesell was heard to remark in the nasal, somewhat precious, and peculiar manner of all Hergesells. Then came a song in German, for which Herr Möller had composed the melody himself. It was a beggar *Lied* and was hailed by the young with stormy applause:

" The beggar lass is a-goin' to the fair —
    Trala-la-la!
The beggar laddie, he means to be there,
    Fol-di-rol, fol-di-rol la! "

Great hilarity prevailed after this merry beggar's song. " How exceptionally good! " said Hergesell again, true to his manner. Something Hungarian followed, also a great hit — rendered in the outlandish original tongue; Möller was undeniably a great success. The professor participated ostentatiously in the applause. This mixture of culture and of historical-retrospective diversion in art, coming into the middle of this shimmy company, warmed his heart. He went up to Möller, congratulated him, and began to discuss the selections, as well as their sources. These were in a song-book with notes, which Möller promised to lend him for his own inspection. Cornelius was the friendlier because, like all fathers, he compared the gifts of strange young men with those of his own son, experiencing various degrees of disquiet, envy, and shame in the process. " There is this Möller," he thought, " an able bank official." (He was by no means certain that Möller displayed great efficiency in the bank.) " And in addition he can show this special talent, to the training of which a good deal of energy and study must have been devoted. Now, there is my poor Bert, who knows nothing and can do nothing, and thinks only of playing the clown, though he hasn't talent even for that! " He strove to be just, and attempted to assure himself that Bert, after all, was a fine boy, perhaps with more good basic qualities than this successful Möller; that possibly there was the making of a great author in him, or something of the sort, and that his Terpsichorean-waiter ambitions were mere boyish will-o'-the-wispishness, a product of the unrestful hour. Still, his envious paternal pessimism was uppermost. When Möller started in to sing once more, Doctor Cornelius went back to his study.

While he continued to work with divided attention, it drew on toward seven o'clock. He thought of a short, matter-of-fact letter which he could write then as well as not. But writing takes time, and when he had finished, it was almost half past seven. The Italian salad was to be served at half past eight, and so it was in order for the professor to go out, get his quantum of fresh air and exercise in the winter darkness, and throw his letters into the post-box. The dance in the hall was once more in full swing. He would be forced to pass through it in order to get to his overcoat and galoshes, but there was no longer anything exciting about this; he had been a frequent auditor of this youthful jollity, and need no longer fear that he might disturb it. He left his study, having first put his papers in order and picked up his letters. He even lingered a little about the hall, for he found his wife seated in an arm-chair close to the door of his room.

She sat looking on, visited from time to time by the Big Ones and other young people. Cornelius stood beside her and likewise regarded the turmoil with a smiling eye, for the merriment had now obviously reached its climax. There were other spectators present. Blue Anna, with all her " rigorous limitations "

46

upon her, stood near the stairs, because the Little Ones had not yet wearied of the festivities and because she was obliged to keep an eye on Biter, for fear of his rotating too violently and thus causing his too turgid blood to boil dangerously. The world below stairs was also bent upon seeing something of the dance and pleasures of the Big Ones. The two Hinterhöfer ladies as well as Xavier were standing in the door that led to the pantry and amusing themselves looking on. Fräulein Walburga, the older of the two *déclassée* sisters and the cooking partner (not to call her the cook, a term she did not like to hear), peered with brown eyes through the thick lenses of her round spectacles, the bridge of which she had wrapped round with a fragment of linen rag in order to keep it from pressing her nose — a genial, good-humoured type. Fräulein Cecilia, the younger, though by no means young, revealed an extremely self-sufficient mien — upholding her dignity as a former member of the third estate. Fräulein Cecilia suffered bitterly over her plunge from this sphere into that of the servant class. She resolutely refused to wear a cap or any other badge or emblem of her profession as a chambermaid. Her greatest ordeal came regularly every Wednesday evening (which was Xavier's night out), when she was forced to serve at table. She would serve

47

with averted face and turned-up nose, a fallen queen. It was sheer torture and grievous oppression to be forced to contemplate her degradation, and once, when the Little Ones were present by chance at the evening meal, both burst simultaneously into loud crying at the sight of her.

Young Xavier knew no such sorrows. He even served very well at table, with a certain natural as well as acquired skill, for he had once been a " *piccolo* " or apprentice in a restaurant. Apart from this, however, he was really a perfect ne'er-do-well and a windbag — with certain positive qualities, to be sure, as his modest master and mistress were ready at all times to acknowledge, but none the less an impossible windbag. One was forced to take him as he was and not expect figs from thistles. He was a product and offspring of the disrupted age, a true specimen of his generation, a servant of the revolutionary epoch, a sympathetic Bolshevist. The professor was in the habit of calling him " Master of Ceremonies," for he proved himself a most useful fellow, obliging and handy, on occasions of special entertainment. But he was totally unacquainted with the notion of duty, and it was as impossible to get him to fulfil the tedious current of daily drudgeries and chores as to teach some dogs to jump over a stick. It was so obviously against his nature that it disarmed one and resigned one to dissatisfaction. He was always ready in the interest of some definite, unusual, and amusing affair to leave his bed at any hour of the night. But he never rose before eight o'clock — he simply would not, would not jump over the stick. But all day long the various expressions of his disrupted existence, the playing of his mouth-organ, his rude but emotional singing, his merry whistling, ascended from the kitchen basement into the upper regions of the house, while the smoke of his cigarettes filled the pantry. He would stand and watch the ladies fallen from high estate, as they worked. In the morning, while the professor was at breakfast, he would tear the leaf off the calendar on the desk, but not do another stroke of work in the room. Doctor Cornelius had ordered him more than once not to tear off the leaves of the calendar, since he was inclined to tear off two leaves at once, and thus ran the risk of creating confusion. But this tearing-off of the leaves had a fascination for young Xavier and he was not going to be done out of it.

Xavier, moreover, was particularly acceptable in that he was a great friend of the children. He would play with the Little Ones in the garden most devotedly, and showed great skill in carving and weaving all kinds of toys for them. At times he would even

49

read to them out of their books, and the accents that fell from his thick lips were wonderful to hear. He was a passionate devotee of the movies, and whenever he had been to a film-play, he would be inclined to melancholy, to vague longings, and to soliloquies. He was moved by an indeterminate hope of one day becoming himself a factor in this magic world, and making his fortune. He based that hope upon his mop of hair and his physical dexterity and recklessness. He would sometimes climb the ash-tree in the front garden, a high but swaying tree, swing himself from branch to branch to the very top, and frighten all who watched him. Having reached the top, he would light a cigarette, swing himself back and forth until the tall trunk shivered to its very roots, and look round for some moving-picture director who might be passing and engage him.

Tonight, if he had taken off his striped jacket and donned civilian clothes, he could easily have joined in the dance without attracting any particular attention. The friends of the Big Ones presented diverse externals; there were several dress-suits in evidence, but these were by no means predominant. Types such as that represented by Möller, the *Liedersänger*, were among them, female as well as male. The professor, who stood beside the arm-chair of his wife and contemplated the picture, was casually familiar with the conditions in which this generation was growing up, and much had come to him through hearsay. These girls were schoolgirls and students, arts-and-crafts workers. The male contingent produced strange adventurous types and existences created solely by the times. There was a pale and weedy youth with pearl studs in his shirt-front, the son of a dentist. He was merely a gambler on Change and was able to live, judging by the stories conveyed to the professor, like a second Aladdin with the magic lamp. He kept an automobile, treated his friends to champagne suppers, and was fond of giving them presents on every occasion, precious little souvenirs of gold and mother of pearl. Today, too, he had brought along certain presents for his young hosts, a gold lead-pencil for Bert and a pair of gigantic ear-rings for Ingrid, real rings and of barbaric size. These, however, thank heaven, were not to be thrust through the lobes of the ears, but merely fastened to them by means of flat-headed little screws. The Big Ones came and displayed their presents laughingly to their parents, who shook their heads wonderingly, whilst Aladdin bowed repeatedly from a distance.

The young people danced with zest, so far as that which took place with such quiet devotion might be called dancing. There was much slow shoving and striding across the carpet, the partners holding each other in new and peculiar ways, the lower part of the body advanced, the shoulders raised, and with a certain swaying of the hips. They did not grow tired, for these movements and steps did not tire. There were no signs of heaving bosoms or of flushed cheeks. Here and there two young girls were dancing together, now and then two young men even — it was all one to them. They strode and stepped to the exotic strains of a gramophone fitted with the loudest needles, which blared forth its fox-trots, shimmies, and one-steps, its double fox, African shimmies, Java dances, and polka creolas — wild perfumed stuff, partly yearning, partly merely exercising, full of an alien rhythm, a monotonous Negro jamboree, tricked out with orchestral effects, percussion notes, tin-panny noises, and odd cluckings.

"What's the name of that record?" Cornelius asked Ingrid as she went skidding by with the pale-faced speculator. The music was not at all bad; it was full of yearning and provoked one to exercise, and certain passages in it rather pleased him.

"*Prince of Pappenheim* — 'Lovely Maiden, Don't Repine!'" she answered, and smiled pleasantly, revealing her white teeth.

52

Cigarette smoke was floating under the chandelier. The fog of festivity had grown thicker — that dry, sweetish, thickish, disturbing festal atmosphere, rich in various ingredients, and so full of memories of early heart-aches, especially for one who had overcome an all too sensitive youth. — The Little Ones were still about; they had been allowed to remain until eight o'clock, since the dance gave them such joy. The young people had accustomed themselves to their taking part; in a way and to a certain extent they " belonged." They had separated by now: Biter was rotating all by himself in his blue velvet tunic in the centre of the carpet; Lorie was comically running behind a sliding couple and trying to hold the gentleman by his dinner-jacket. It was Max Hergesell, with his partner, the Plaichinger girl. They were doing these slidings and glidings very well; it was a pleasure to look at them. One was forced to concede that the dances of the wild new times were capable of being converted into something quite agreeable, when the right people did the converting. Young Hergesell took the lead in an admirable manner, moving freely, and yet, as it seemed, keeping within the rules. How elegantly he executed the backward steps, whenever there was room! But even in a crush he was able to maintain himself in the best taste, supported by the

suppleness of a partner who had developed the astonishing grace which women of a full figure are sometimes able to command. They were talking face to
face and did not appear to be observing Lorie, who
was following them. Others were laughing over the
persistence of the little one, and Doctor Cornelius
sought to capture her as she passed and to draw her
to him. But Lorie disengaged herself with a tortured
expression, and wanted nothing to do with Abel for
the time being. She refused to recognize him, braced
her little arms against his breast, and, averting her
little face, struggled to get away from him, nervous
and irritated, bent on following her caprice.

The professor experienced a sharp pang, and at
that moment hated the party, which bewildered the
heart of his darling and alienated it. His love, this
love so strange and unconjecturable in its roots and
origins, was very sensitive. He smiled mechanically,
but his eyes lost their light and settled into a fixed
stare upon a pattern in the carpet, between the feet of
the dancing couples.

" The Little Ones ought to go to bed! " he said to
his wife. But she begged for another quarter-hour for
the children. They had been promised that, because
they were enjoying the turmoil so greatly. He smiled
again and shook his head, remained standing there a

moment longer, and then went into the cloak-room, which was overflowing with coats, scarfs, hats, and overshoes.

He had difficulty in dragging his own things out of the confusion. And then Max Hergesell came into the cloak-room, wiping his forehead with his handkerchief.

"Herr Professor," he began in the tone common to all Hergesells, and with a certain youthful reverence, "I see you are going out. These pumps of mine are the limit, they pinch like the very Old Nick. They are really too small for me, as I've discovered, quite apart from their hardness. This presses here, so frightfully, on my big-toe-nail," he went on, standing on one foot, while he held the other in his hand, "that I can't stand it. I've made up my mind to change back into my street shoes. — But wait — can't I give you a hand?"

"Thank you," said Cornelius. "Don't worry about me! You must get rid of your own troubles! It's awfully kind of you." For Hergesell had knelt down and had fastened the clasps of the professor's overshoes.

The professor thanked him again, agreeably affected by so much sincere and respectful solicitude. "You must go and enjoy yourself," he said, "after you have changed your shoes! It's impossible that you should continue to dance in shoes that pinch. You simply must change them. *Auf wiedersehen!* — I must get out for a breath of fresh air."

" I'm going now to have another dance with Lorie," Hergesell called after him. " She'll be a star dancer some day, when she's old enough. You can bank on that! "

" You think so? " Cornelius asked, standing at the house door. " Well, you are an expert, a champion. But see that you don't get curvature of the spine bending down to her! "

He waved his hand and went out. " Nice boy," he thought, as he left the garden. " A student of engineering, sees his way clearly — everything in order there. And then so good-looking and pleasant." And he was once more seized by paternal envy, because of his " poor Bert " — by strange perturbations which caused him to see the life of this young stranger in the rosiest light, and that of his son in the most dismal. In such a mood he began his evening walk.

He went up the boulevard, crossed the bridge, and then walked up-stream for a bit, along the river promenade to the third bridge. It was wet and cold, and now and then there was a flurry of snow. He had turned up the collar of his overcoat, and held his cane against his back, the crook hooked over one forearm, and now and again he drew deep breaths of the wintry evening air. His mind wandered to learned matters, as usual during these walks, to his lecture at the university, to the sentences that he was going to utter tomorrow in relation to Philip's battle against the revolutionary tendency of the Germanic spirit, sentences which were to be packed with justice and melancholy. Especially with justice, he thought. Justice was the soul of scholarship, the principle of knowledge and of light, and the young people must be shown them in this relationship, not only because of the intellectual discipline, but for human and personal reasons — in order not to offend them nor to antagonize their political opinions, which today, of course, were terribly split up and full of contrarieties; it had all resulted in heaping up a good deal of explosive matter. To draw down the disapproval of one side was easy, and even to cause a scandal, should one take sides in an historical matter. But taking sides, he thought, was also unhistorical; justice alone was historical. Only, to be sure, for that very reason and rightly considered — justice was not hot-blooded youth nor fresh, adventurous faith and resolution; it was melancholy. But as it was melancholy by nature, it naturally and secretly sympathized with the melancholy, the hopeless part — with historical power

57

more than with what is fresh, adventurous, and reso-
lute. Was it possible that in the last analysis this
justice consisted of such sympathy and could not exist
without it? And possibly, after all, justice did not
exist? the professor asked himself, and was so absorbed in this thought that he threw his letters into
the letter-box at the bridge almost unconsciously and
began to walk back. The thought he had awakened
and pursued was a thought disturbing to learning,
but the thought itself was part of science, learning,
and scholarship, a theme for the intellect and conscience and psychology, and he was in duty bound
to accept it without prejudice, whether it disturbed
him or not. — It was with such musings that Doctor
Cornelius returned home.

Xavier was standing in the arch of the front entrance, apparently on the look-out for him.

" Herr Professor," said Xavier, in his rich Bava-
rian accent, moving his thick lips in the dark and
giving a toss to his hair, " you'd better go right up and
see Lorie. It's terrible; she's gone all to pieces."

" What's the matter? " asked Cornelius, frightened. " Is she ill? "

" No, not exactly," replied Xavier. " But she's upset all right, cryin' her eyes out. It's about the gent
that danced with her, that one in the dinner-coat, Herr

Hergesell. We couldn't get her out of the hall, not a one of us, and she cried and cried — bucketfuls. She's all broke up — it's terrible! "

" Nonsense," said the professor, who had stepped into the house and tossed his things into the cloak-room. He said nothing further, opened the curtained glass door to the hall, and without even so much as a glance at the company hurried up the stairs to the right. He took the stairs two at a time and hurried across the upper hall and another small space directly into the nursery, followed by Xavier, who stayed at the door.

The nursery was brightly illuminated. There was a gaily coloured paper frieze that ran around the walls, there was a big set of shelves filled with a confusion of toys, a rocking-horse with red-varnished nostrils braced its hoofs against its curved rockers, and other toys — a small trumpet, building-blocks, railroad cars — lay scattered upon the linoleum of the floor. The little white beds with their straight railings stood quite close together: Lorie's in the corner near the window, and Biter's a yard from it, both projecting into the room.

Biter was sleeping. As usual he had said his prayers in a loud vibrant voice with the assistance of Blue Anna, and had then fallen instantly into that

59

stormy, red-glowing, tremendously deep sleep from which not even a cannon-shot fired off beside his couch could wake him. His clenched fists, thrown back upon the pillow, were resting on both sides of his head, close to that little wig of his, ruffled by vehement sleep and all tangled and awry.

Lorie's bed was surrounded by women. There was Blue Anna and there were the Hinterhöfer ladies, standing about the railing of the bed, consulting together. They stepped aside as the professor drew near and he saw Lorie sitting against the middle of her little pillow, pale and sobbing. She cried as Doctor Cornelius had never known her to cry. Her beautiful little hands were resting on the counterpane before her; her little night-gown, trimmed with a narrow edging of lace, had slipped down from her birdlike, slight little shoulders. Her head, that sweet little head that Cornelius so loved, because with the projecting lower part of the face resting upon the thin neck it always reminded him of a flower upon its stem, was inclined to one side, so that her tearful eyes were directed at the angle of the wall and the ceiling. Her huge burden of grief seemed somehow to lie in the same direction, for she kept nodding towards it constantly. Whether as a result of deliberate and conscious expression or as a result of the convulsive movements of sobbing, her little head nodded and shook without ever stopping. Her mobile mouth, however, with its Cupid's bow of an upper lip, was half open like that of a tiny *mater dolorosa,* and while the tears poured from her eyes, she uttered monotonous little sounds of woe, sounds which had nothing in common with the angry and superfluous crying of naughty children, but which originated in some real heart-ache. The professor, who could not bear to see Lorie weep in any circumstances, but who had never seen her weep thus, was wrung with an all but insupportable pity. This pity, however, found its first expression in a sharp and nervous *volte-face* towards the two Hinterhöfer sisters.

" I am sure," he said, with more or less feeling, " that there is plenty to do in getting dinner ready. But it seems that it's left to the mistress to do by herself? "

This sufficed for the finely attuned ears of persons who had once belonged to the middle classes. With a sense of genuine injury they removed themselves, being mocked at in addition by Xavier as they swept through the doorway. For Xavier happened to be born of low estate to start with, and the condition of the fallen dames was a source of perpetual amusement to him.

".Dear, darling Lorie," said Cornelius in a

strained voice, as he folded the suffering little thing in his arms and sat down in a chair beside her small bed. " What's the matter with my little girl? "

Her tears were falling on his face.

" Abel — Abel," she sobbed and stammered, " why — isn't — Max — my brother? Max — ought — to be my brother."

What a catastrophe, what wretchedness! All the result of the dance and its dangerous psychological possibilities! thought Cornelius, as he glanced up at Blue Anna, who, with her hands folded upon her apron, stood, the very picture of dignified limitation, at the foot of the cot.

" It's a case," she said, severely and oracularly, drawing in her under lip, " of that there child having her feminine instincts so strongly developed."

" Hold your tongue! " answered Cornelius, greatly troubled. He was forced to be content that Lorie did not draw away from him, or thrust him from her, as she had done before in the hall, but clung to him as though seeking help, while she repeated her foolish, distraught wish that Max might be her brother, and desperately demanded to be allowed to go down to him, to the hall, that he might dance with her. But Max was dancing in the hall with the Plaichinger girl, who was a fully developed valkyrie and had legitimate rights to him — whereas Lorie, to the compassionate heart of the professor, had never seemed so frail or so birdlike as just then, pressing herself against him, helpless and shaken by sobs, unaware of what had invaded her poor little soul. She knew nothing of this. It was not clear to her that the plump, full-grown, and duly authorized Plaichinger girl was the cause of her sufferings — the girl that was permitted to dance with Max Hergesell, while Lorie, though incomparably the more lovely of the two, had been permitted to do so only once and that once only in sport. But it was impossible to reproach young Hergesell for that, for it would have implied an insane imputation. Lorie's grief was incurable and without rights and should have hidden itself. But as it was a grief without understanding, it was also a grief without inhibition, and this produced a great pain. Blue Anna and Xavier were not at all concerned about this pain; they showed that they were impervious to it, either out of stupidity or a matter-of-fact naturalness. But the paternal heart of the professor was lacerated by this misery, by the humiliating terrors of this passion, without rights and without cure.

There was no use in telling poor Lorie that she had a splendid little brother in the person of Biter, who was sleeping so strenuously close by. Through her tears she merely threw a contemptuous and painful look at the cot beside her own and called for Max. Nor was there any use in promising her an extensive " five-gentlemen " promenade round the dining-room, nor was there consolation in the glowing description he gave of the wonderful thoroughness with which the cushion game would be carried out before lunch. She refused to listen to any of this, refused to consider all admonitions to lie down and go to sleep. She did not want to go to sleep, she wanted to sit up and suffer. — And then both of them, Abel as well as Lorie, suddenly caught themselves listening to something wonderful that was now happening, something that was approaching the nursery step by step, double step by double step, and which then overpoweringly put in appearance.

It was Xavier's work — that was clear at once. Xavier had not remained standing in the doorway, after he had mocked the two expelled lady-helps. He had got under way, he had become enterprising, he had made his arrangements. He had gone down into the hall, had plucked Max Hergesell by the sleeve, whispered something to him with his thick lips, and begged him to do something. And there they both were. Xavier once more took up his station at the door, for he had done his part; but Max Hergesell came straight through the rooms towards Lorie's bed, clad in his dinner-jacket, with his dark little side-burns by his ears, and his handsome black eyes — came like one visibly conscious of his role as a bearer of happiness, a fairy prince and Lohengrin, as one who says: " Well, here I am, all trouble will now be over." Cornelius was almost as amazed as Lorie.

" Just look," he said feebly, " who's here. Isn't it nice of Herr Hergesell? "

" It isn't nice of him at all! " said Hergesell. " It stands to reason, doesn't it, that I should have another look at my partner and want to say good-night to her? "

Then he stepped up to the cot, within which the now silent Lorie sat. She smiled blissfully through her tears. A tiny, high little note, a half-suppressed sob of happiness, came from her lips, and then she gazed silently up at her noble knight-errant, gazed at him with her golden eyes, which, though red and swollen, were so incomparably more beautiful than those of the buxom Plaichinger damsel. She did not lift her arms to embrace him. Her happiness, like her sorrow, was without understanding, but that she did not do. Her pretty little hands remained quietly resting upon the counterpane, while Max Hergesell leaned his arms upon the rail of the cot, as upon the balustrade of a balcony.

" ' Just so she need not,' " he said, " ' sit weeping on her lonely bed throughout the sorrow-laden nights.' " And he stole a glance at the professor, that he might win applause for this highly apropos quotation from Goethe. " Ah, ha, ha! " He laughed outright. " At her age! 'Lovely maiden, don't repine! ' You are a dear! You'll do, little one. You need only remain as you are. Ha ha! At this age! You see, I've come now. You go to sleep, little Lorie. And don't you cry any more."

Lorie looked at him, transfigured. Her small bird-like shoulder was bare; the professor pulled the little lace hem over it. He was forced to think of a sentimental story, of a dying child to whom a clown is brought, one she had remembered with inexpugnable ecstasy from the circus. The clown, clad in his costume, came to the child in its dying hour, a clown embroidered with silver butterflies before and behind, and the child died happy. Max Hergesell was not embroidered, and Lorie, thank God, was not about to die — she had merely " gone to pieces " ; but otherwise there was a certain pertinence to the story, a certain relation, and the emotions which the professor felt for young Hergesell, who stood there and gabbled idioti-

66

cally, more for the father than the child — something which Lorie, however, did not notice — were a strange mixture of gratitude, embarrassment, hatred, and admiration.

" Good-night, my little Lorelei! " said Hergesell and held out his hand across the railing of the bed. Her tiny, pretty, white little hand vanished within his large, strong, reddish one. " Sleep well," he said. " Pleasant dreams! But not about me! Heaven forbid! At your age! Ha, ha, ha, ha! " And thus he concluded his fairy-clown visit and was escorted by Cornelius to the door.

" Don't mention it," he said. " Not another word! " — such was his polite, magnanimous way of warding off the professor's thanks on the way to the door. Xavier followed him, in order to start serving the Italian salad downstairs.

Doctor Cornelius went back to Lorie, who had now snuggled down, resting her cheek upon her flat little pillow.

" Well, that was nice! " he said, as he gently smoothed the coverlet over her, and she nodded with a deep half-sobbing intake of breath. He sat there for at least a quarter of an hour longer and watched her go to sleep, watched her drop off the way her little brother had gone to sleep, though so much sooner. Her silken, brown hair took on the lovely tumble of ring-lets which it always fell into when she slept; the long lashes lay close upon her eyes, from which so much grief had streamed; the angelic mouth with the arched and curving upper lip was open in sweet contentment, and only an occasional tiny, half-suppressed after-sob trembled through her slow, even breathing.

Her little hands, her rosy-white, flower-like hands — how still they lay there, the one upon the blue cov-erlet of the bed, the other in front of her face on the pillow! The heart of Doctor Cornelius was surcharged with tenderness, as with wine.

How fortunate, he thought, that every breath she draws in sleep lets Lethe pour into her little soul — that the night of a child establishes so broad and deep an abyss between one day and the next! Tomorrow, he knew, young Hergesell would be only a pale shadow to her, powerless to cause her heart a tremor, and her joy, disembarrassed of memories, would be perfect as she played at the " five-gentlemen " promenade and the fascinating cushion game with Abel and Biter.

Thank Heaven for that!

1926

HOW JAPPE
FOUGHT DO ESCOBAR

HOW JAPPE FOUGHT DO ESCOBAR

I WAS greatly startled when Johnny Bishop told me that Jappe and Do Escobar wanted to fight each other and that we should go and look on.

It was during the summer holidays, in Travemünde, on a broiling hot day, with a faint land breeze and a flat, wide-ebbing sea. We had been some three-quarters of an hour in the water and were lying under the boards and beams of the bath-house on the firm sand, together with Jürgen Brattström, the son of the ship-owner. Johnny and Brattström lay upon their backs, completely naked. I found it more comfortable to keep my towel wrapped about my hips. Brattström asked me why I did this, and as I had no proper answer forthcoming, Johnny remarked with that winning and winsome smile of his that I was very likely a bit too big to lie about naked. I was actually larger and more developed than he and Brattström, and also, no doubt, a little older — about thirteen. And so I swallowed Johnny's explanation in silence, even though it implied something derogatory to me. For in

Johnny's company it was easy to cut a comic figure if one happened to be a little less small, a little less delicate and childlike in body than himself, who was all these things to such a high degree. He would then look up at one with his pretty, blue, girlish eyes with an expression at once friendly and full of smiling mockery, as though he would say: " What an overgrown lout you have already become! " The ideal of manliness and long trousers lost its effect in his presence, and this at a time, not long after the war, when strength, courage, and every kind of rude virtue stood in high esteem among us boys, and all kinds of things were considered effeminate. But Johnny, as a foreigner, or half a foreigner, was quite free from this influence. On the contrary there was something about him that reminded one of a woman who has preserved herself well and who is able to make merry at others who are less skilled in this respect. He was also by a long way the only boy in town who was dressed in an elegant and markedly aristocratic manner; that is to say, in genuine English sailor-suits with blue linen collars, sailor's knots, cords, a silver whistle in his breast-pocket, and an anchor upon the puffy sleeves, which narrowed to a band at the wrists. All this would have been regarded as dandified in any other lad, and punished accordingly. But he carried it off charmingly and as a matter of course, took no harm from it, and was never forced to suffer from it in the slightest.

He looked like a thin little Cupid as he lay there, his arms upraised, his pretty, long, English head, with its soft, blond locks, bedded in his small hands. His father had been a German merchant who had naturalized himself in England and who had died some years before. But his mother was a born Englishwoman, a lady of mild and quiet character, with a longish face, who had settled in our town with her children — Johnny and a little girl who was quite as pretty, even though a bit tricky. The mother always went dressed exclusively in black, in constant mourning for her husband, and no doubt she honoured his last wishes in letting the children grow up in Germany. She was evidently in good circumstances. She owned a spacious house just outside the city, and a villa at the seaside; and from time to time she would make trips to distant health resorts with Johnny and Sissie. She did not belong to society, though all doors would have been open to her. She lived in the utmost retirement, either because of her mourning, or because the horizon of our leading families was too narrow for her. But by means of invitations, and by arranging games in common, by Johnny's and Sissie's participation in dancing and deportment classes and

73

such like, she provided company for her children, and though she did not herself choose this company, she nevertheless supervised it with quiet solicitude, and in such a way that Johnny and Sissie came into touch only with children of well-to-do houses. This, to be sure, was not the result of a fixed principle, and yet it was a simple fact. Frau Bishop also contributed to my own education, even at a distance, in that she taught me that in order to be respected by others it is only necessary to respect oneself. Though deprived of its masculine head, the little family showed none of the stigmata of neglect and decline which so often arouse middle-class suspicion in similar cases. Without any train of relatives, without a title, or tradition, influence, or public position, her life was at once aloof and self-assured, and firmly and deliberately self-assured to such a degree that every concession was made to her silently and unhesitatingly, and the friendship of her children was held in high esteem by both boys and girls.

As to Jürgen Brattström, his father had only recently risen to a position of wealth and public offices and had built the red sandstone house for himself and his family in the Burgfeld, which made him a neighbour of Frau Bishop's. Thus, with Frau Bishop's quiet sanction, Jürgen had become Johnny's garden playmate and companion on the way to school — a phleg-matic, officious, short-limbed lad without any domi-nant characteristics. He was already carrying on a little surreptitious trade in licorice.

As I have said, I was exceedingly startled by Johnny's communication about the impending battle between Jappe and Do Escobar, which was to be fought that day in deadly earnest on the Leuchtenfeld at twelve o'clock. This might prove most terrible, for Jappe and Escobar were strong, daring fellows with a knightly code of honour, and a hostile encounter between them might well arouse anxiety. In memory they still appear to me as big and manly as at that time, although they could not have been older than fifteen. Jappe came from a middle-class family of the town; he was taken very little care of and he was really almost what we called a " butcher " at that time, a dare-devil, although with a touch of the man about town. Do Escobar was very free by nature, an exotic alien, who did not even attend school regularly, but merely came as a kind of outsider to listen (a dis-orderly but paradisal life!) — one who boarded with some burgher's family and who rejoiced in absolute independence. Both were individuals who went to bed late, visited taverns, went loafing along the Breiten-strasse in the evening, followed girls, did reckless things on the cross-bars — in short, they were "sports." Although they did not stay at the Kurhotel at Travemünde — where they would scarcely have belonged — but lodged somewhere in the town, in the Kurgarten itself they acted the part of men of the world. And I knew that in the evening — that is, Sundays — long after I was lying in my bed in one of the Swiss cottages and had peacefully dropped off to slumber amid the strains of the Kurhaus concert, they as well as other members of the gay young world went strolling adventurously to and fro in the tide of summer visitors and excursionists, past the long tent of the confectioner, seeking adult acquaintance and finding it. In doing this they had crossed each other's path — God knows why or how. It is possible that they may only have bumped into each other as they slouched past and, being quick in the matter of injured honour, had made a *casus belli* of the incident. Johnny, who of course had also been asleep long before and who had heard of the quarrel only through hearsay, declared in his agreeable, somewhat veiled, and childish voice that the trouble had very likely arisen over a "wench," and this was not at all difficult to suppose of such audacious up-to-dateness as characterized Jappe and Do Escobar. In short, they had not made any scene in public, but in curt and sardonic words

76

had agreed on the place and hour for settling this point of honour. Tomorrow at twelve o'clock they would meet at such and such a place upon the Leuchtenfeld. Good-evening! Herr Knaak of Hamburg, ballet-master, *maître de plaisir,* and manager of the " reunions " in the Kurhaus had been present and had agreed to come to the duelling-ground.

Johnny was wholly delighted at the prospect of the fight, and neither he nor Brattström shared the nervousness I felt. He repeatedly assured us, forming his *R's,* according to his charming habit, by means of his gums, that the two would fight each other in deadly seriousness and as real enemies, and then with an amused and rather sarcastic matter-of-factness he debated the chances of victory. Jappe and Do Escobar were both dreadfully strong — huh! Both of them powerful bullies. It was amusing that they would now for once solemnly settle which of the two was the more powerful bully. Jappe, Johnny declared, had a broad chest and first-rate muscles of the arms and legs, as one might observe daily when he bathed. But Do Escobar was extraordinarily sinewy and violent, so that it was difficult to predict who would win the upper hand. It was strange to hear Johnny expressing himself in such a superior manner as to the qualities of Jappe and Do Escobar and at the same time to see his

77

own feeble childish arms, which would never have served him for either striking or warding off a blow.

As to myself, I certainly had no intention of refraining from visiting the scene of combat. That would have been absurd, and besides, what was about to happen attracted me mightily. I was certainly obliged to go and look at everything, now that I had heard all about it — that was a kind of moral obligation, which, however, was forced to contend hardily with other rebellious emotions: with a great shyness and shame, unpugnacious and faint of heart as I was, to venture upon the scene of such virile deeds; a nervous fear of the upheavals which the sight of a grim battle, in dead earnest and, so to speak, to the death, might provoke in me. These upheavals I experienced in anticipation, and also a simple, craven fear that, once there and tarred with the same brush, I might be exposed to demands and challenges which were repugnant to my inmost nature, an anxiety that I might be forced to prove that I too on my part was a dashing fellow, something which I abhorred more than anything. On the other hand, I could not help putting myself in Jappe's and Do Escobar's place, and inwardly feeling the devastating emotions which I presupposed in them. I imagined the insult and the challenge in the Kurgarten, and with them I suppressed, for reasons of elegance and *savoir faire*, the urge to start pummelling with my fists. I experienced the passion of their indignant, outraged sense of justice, the grief, the throbbing, brain-searing hate, the attacks of raving impatience and revenge amidst which they must have spent the night. Then, driven to extremes, and borne beyond all timorousness, I began in spirit to fight blindly and bloodily with an opponent just as dehumanized as myself, drove my fist into his hateful mouth with all the power at my command, so that all his teeth were shattered, received in return a brutal kick in the abdomen, and went down in red waves, whereupon I awoke in my bed, with quieted nerves and ice-packings amidst the gentle reproaches of my family. In short, when it got to be half past eleven and we got up to dress ourselves, I was half exhausted by excitement, and in the dressing-room, as well as afterwards when we left the bathing-establishment fully dressed, my heart beat just as though it were I who was to fight Jappe or Do Escobar, in public and under arduous conditions.

I still remember perfectly how we three went down the narrow plank gangway which led up from the beach to the bathing-establishment. We hopped, of course, so as to make the gangway sway up and down and let us balance upon it, as upon a spring-board.

Having reached the sands, we did not follow the board-walk which ran along the beach between the pavilions and the wicker beach-chairs, but struck inland, somewhat in the direction of the Kurhaus, but a little more to the left. The sun brooded upon the sand-dunes and coaxed a dry and heated fragrance from the sand-thistles and the reeds which grew in the sparse and arid soil and pricked our legs. Nothing was to be heard save the uninterrupted buzzing of horse-flies of a metallic blue, which apparently stood immovably in the heavy heat, and then suddenly changed their position and resumed their sharp and monotonous song in another place. The cooling effect of the bath was long since past. Brattström and I now and then took off our head-coverings — he his Swedish skipper's cap with its projecting visor of oil-cloth, I my round Heligoland woollen cap, a so-called tam-o'-shanter — and mopped the sweat from our foreheads. Johnny suffered very little from the heat, thanks to his thinness, and no doubt also because his clothes were more elegantly adapted to the summer weather than our own. He walked on between Brattström and me, clad in his light and comfortable sailor's suit of striped washable goods, his throat and calves bare, his blue sailor's cap, with its short ribbons and its English inscription, perched upon his

80

pretty little head, his long and slender feet in white kid ties with scarcely a trace of heel. And so he walked with a lengthy, climbing stride and with knees that seemed a little crooked, and with that agreeable accent of his sang a popular song, " O Little Fisher Maiden! " which was current at that time, sang it with an indecent variation, which had been invented by the precocious youth. That was the way he was: despite all his childishness, he already knew various things and was not at all too squeamish to speak of them. But then he would put on a light hypocritical mien and say: " Shame! one ought not to sing such nasty songs! " and pretend that it was we and not himself who had so salaciously apostrophized the little fisher maiden.

I myself had not the slightest inclination for singing, for we were already close to the place of rendezvous and the fateful theatre of combat. The sharp grass of the sand-dunes had changed to sandy moss, to a kind of meagre meadow land — this was the Leuchtenfeld which we were traversing, so named after the round, yellow lighthouse tower which lifted itself at a considerable distance to the left — and so quite unexpectedly we arrived at our goal.

It was a warm and peaceful place, very little frequented by people and hidden from view by brushwood willows. In the clearing within the line of willow-bushes were sitting and lying a group of young people in a circle, like a living barricade, nearly all of them older than we, and belonging to various classes of society. Apparently we were the last spectators to arrive. They were only waiting for ballet-master Knaak, who was to attend the fight as a neutral and as umpire. Both Jappe and Do Escobar were at hand — I saw them at once. They sat in the circle at some distance from each other, and each pretended to be unaware of the other's existence. After we had greeted a few acquaintances by silent nods, we too sat down upon the warm earth, drawing our legs under us.

There was smoking. Even Jappe and Do Escobar had cigarettes in the corners of their mouths, and as they sat there, blinking in the smoke and each closing one eye, it was clear to all that they had a certain appreciation of the grandeur of being able to sit there thus and smoke a cigarette with such nonchalance, just before the battle. Both were already dressed in adult fashion, but Do Escobar in a far more man-of-the-world fashion than Jappe. He wore tan shoes with very pointed toes to go with his light-grey summer suit, a rose-coloured shirt with attached cuffs, a gay-coloured silk tie, and a round, small-brimmed straw hat, pushed back upon his head, so that the thick, firm, shiny black, well-oiled hillock of hair — for he had brushed it up sideways across his forehead to make this eminence — showed under the hat. Now and then he lifted and shook his right hand, so that the silver bracelet he wore might slip back under his cuff. Jappe looked far less pretentious. His legs were enclosed in tight trousers, which were lighter than his coat and waistcoat and fastened under his black boots by means of straps. The checked sports-cap which covered his blond hair he had, in contrast to Do Escobar, drawn far down over his forehead. He squatted upon the ground and embraced his knees with his arms, and one could then observe, first, that he wore loose cuffs over the sleeves of his shirt, and, second, that the nails of his entwined fingers were cut far too short, or that he was addicted to the vice of gnawing them off. The mood that prevailed in the group was serious and, despite the jaunty and independent pose of smoking, embarrassed and in the main silent. The only one who rebelled against this was Do Escobar himself, who kept on speaking to his entourage, in a loud, hoarse voice with rolling *Rs* whirling off his tongue, and blowing the smoke through his nostrils. His rattling manner revolted me, and I felt inclined to side with Jappe in spite of his all too short finger-nails. Jappe merely passed a word now and then over his shoulder with his neighbours, and seemed apparently quite composed, as he followed the smoke of his cigarette with his eyes.

And then Herr Knaak arrived. I still see him advance with elastic steps from the direction of the Kurhaus, clad in his morning suit of blue striped flannel, and, raising his straw hat, remain standing just beyond our circle. I do not believe that he came very willingly; rather, I am convinced that he made the best of a bad job, by lending his presence to a fist-fight; but his position, his difficult relation to the belligerent and pronouncedly masculine youth of the place, no doubt forced him to accede. Brown-skinned, handsome, and fat (fat especially in the region of the hips), he gave lessons in dancing and deportment during the winter, not only privately in families, but also publicly in the Casino, and during the summer he fulfilled the functions of an arranger of festivals and a commissioner of baths at the Kurhaus at Travemünde. What with his vain eyes, his elastic, rhythmical walk — he would always carefully set the out-turned toes of his boots first upon the ground and then let the ball of the foot follow — with his self-satisfied and studied manner of speech, the theatrical self-assurance of his address, the impossible, demonstrative finickiness of

84

his manners, he proved the delight of the female sex, whereas the masculine world, especially the critical juvenile section, regarded him sceptically.

I have often thought of the position in life occupied by François Knaak and have always found it strange and fantastic. The son of simple parents, such as he was, he stood poised, as it were, in mid-air by his very cultivation of the highest forms of human intercourse, and though he did not belong to society, he was appointed the guardian and teacher of its moral ideals, and paid accordingly. Jappe and Do Escobar were also pupils of his, not private pupils like Johnny, Brattström, and me, but in his public classes at the Casino; and it was there that the ways and character of Herr Knaak suffered the most rigorous criticism at the hands of the young people — for we of the private lessons were more mildly disposed. A fellow who taught how one was to behave nicely to little girls, a fellow concerning whom there were unconsidered rumours that he wore a corset, who seized the edge of his frock-coat with his finger-tips, bent the knee, cut caprioles, and then leaped suddenly into the air, where he twinkled with his feet and then plumped back elastically upon the parquetry — well, was such a fellow a man at all? Such was the suspicion that burdened Herr Knaak's person and destiny, and this was aggravated precisely by his excessive assurance and superiority. His advantage in years was great and it was said (a most amusing idea!) that he had a wife and children in Hamburg. This attribute of his as an adult and the circumstance that one met him only in the dance-hall saved him from being caught and unmasked. Could he do athletics? Had he ever been able to do them? Had he courage? Had he strength? In short, was he to be regarded as a gentleman? He had no chance for manifesting any of the more respectable qualities, qualities which might have balanced his drawing-room arts and conferred respectability upon him. But there were boys who went about and simply called him an ape and a coward. He was apparently aware of this, and it was for this reason that he had come today — in order to proclaim his interest in a real fight and to act as a comrade to the young people, even though his office as bathing-commissioner should have prevented him from tolerating this illegal recourse to the code of honour. But it was my conviction that he did not feel very comfortable in this position, and that he was clearly conscious of having trodden on dangerous ground. Several of the spectators measured him with cold eyes and he himself peered anxiously about to see if people might be coming.

He excused himself politely for his belated arrival. A discussion with the directors of the Kurhaus in connexion with the "reunion" on Saturday evening had detained him. "Are the combatants on hand?" he then asked in a firm voice. "Then we can begin." Leaning on his cane and crossing his feet, he stood outside our circle, began gnawing his brown moustache with his lower lip, and narrowed his eyes darkly like an expert.

Jappe and Do Escobar stood up, threw away their cigarettes, and began to make ready for the fight. Do Escobar did so with most impressive swiftness and dispatch. He threw his hat, his jacket and waistcoat upon the ground, unloosed his cravat, unbuttoned his collar and suspenders, and cast them upon the same pile. He even pulled his rose-coloured shirt with attached cuffs out of his trousers, wriggled nimbly out of the sleeves, and stood there in a red and white striped under-shirt with short sleeves which revealed his tawny arms, already covered with black hair, bare to the middle of his biceps.

"At your service, sir," he said, rolling his *R's*, and stepped swiftly into the centre of the field, throwing out his chest and adjusting his shoulder-blades with a jerk. He had kept on his silver bracelet.

Jappe, who was not yet ready, turned his head towards him, and with raised brows and eyelids almost closed, looked at his feet for a moment, as though he would say: " Be so good as to wait. I'll come all right, even without those monkey-shines of yours." Although he was broader in the shoulders, he did not appear half so athletic and fit for the fight as Do Escobar, as he stood up to him. His legs, in the tight-fitting breeches with the strap, were knock-kneed, and his soft shirt, already somewhat yellowed, with the wide sleeves closed at the wrists by plain pearl buttons, and crossed by grey elastic suspenders, looked like nothing, whilst Do Escobar's striped under-shirt and especially the black hairs upon his arms conveyed an extraordinarily pugnacious and dangerous impression. Both were pale, but this was more noticeable in Jappe, because he usually had red cheeks. He had the face of a merry and rather brutal tow-head with a pug-nose, covered with a sprinkling of freckles. Do Escobar's nose, on the other hand, was short, straight, and inclined to droop, and there was a dark trace of moustache upon his pouting upper lip.

They stood with hanging arms almost chest to chest and each stared at the abdominal region of the other with sinister and contemptuous mien. It was obvious that they did not know what they were to do with each other, and that was what I, too, distinctly felt. Since their encounter a whole night and half a day had elapsed and the zest for hammering each other, which had been so active only the night before and which had been bridled only by their chivalrousness, had had time to cool off. And now at a fixed hour, in cold blood and in the face of an assembled audience, they were supposed, at a word of command, to do that which they would so gladly have done yesterday out of sheer living impulse. And finally, after all, they were well-behaved boys and not ancient gladiators. Calm reason surely induces a human reluctance to pummel somebody's sound body to pieces with one's fists. Such were my thoughts and such, no doubt, was the truth.

But as something had to be done for sheer honour's sake, they began to prod each other's chests with the ends of their five outspread fingers, as though they believed, in mutual contempt, that each could level his opponent to the ground by so slight an effort, and also with the obvious intention of irritating each other. The moment, however, that Jappe's face began to contort itself, Do Escobar broke off this preliminary skirmish.

"I beg your pardon, sir," said he, as he retreated two steps and turned aside. He did this in order to draw the buckle at the back of his trousers tighter, for he had taken off his braces, and, as he was narrow in the hips, it is likely that his trousers had begun to slip down. After he had once more girded up his loins, he uttered some rattling phrase, something gummy, something Spanish, which no one understood and which was no doubt meant to signify that he was now readier than ever, threw back his shoulders once more, and stepped forward. It was clear that he was supremely vain.

The skirmishing with shoulders and open hands began again. But suddenly, quite unexpectedly, there was a short, blind, violent tussle, a whirling mix-up of fists, which lasted three seconds and which then broke off just as suddenly.

" Now they're in form," said Johnny, who sat beside me and held a dry grass-stalk in his mouth. " I'll bet you that Jappe will get the best of him. Do Escobar is too showy. Just see! he is always squinting at the other! Jappe has himself well in hand. Will you bet that he'll lick him to a finish? "

They had rebounded from each other and now stood with heaving chests, and with fists braced against their hips. Both, certainly, had taken a good blow or two, for their faces had grown wicked, and both protruded their lips with an indignant air, as much as to say: " What do you mean by hurting me that way? "

Jappe's eyes were red, and Do Escobar showed his white teeth, as they once more started in.

They now pummelled each other with all their might, alternately, and after brief pauses, upon the shoulders, the forearms, and the breast.

"That's nothing," said Johnny in his sweet voice. "They'll never finish each other that way. They ought to hit each other under the chin, an upper cut under the chin. That settles it."

In the mean time Do Escobar had seized both of Jappe's arms with his left arm, holding them against his chest as in a vice, and with his right fist he belaboured Jappe's ribs incessantly.

This caused a great commotion. "No clenching!" shouted a number of the spectators and leaped to their feet. Herr Knaak, with a frightened face, rushed into the middle of the "ring." "No clenching!" he too shouted. "You are clenching, my dear friend! That is against the rules!" He separated them and once more admonished Do Escobar that clenching was absolutely forbidden. And then he once more withdrew behind the periphery.

Jappe was furious — that was plain to see. He was very pale and kept massaging his side, at the same time looking at Do Escobar and nodding his head slowly in a manner that boded no good. And when the next round began, his face bore an expression of such determination that all were sure that he would give the decisive blow.

And, really, as soon as the new encounter had begun, Jappe executed a coup — made use of a feint, which he had apparently thought out beforehand. A feint with the left towards the head caused Do Escobar to cover his face, but no sooner had he done this than Jappe's right landed so hard in the region of the solar plexus that Do Escobar doubled up and his face took on the aspect of yellow wax.

" That went home," said Johnny. " That hurts. And now it's possible that he'll pull himself together and go at it in earnest, so as to get even."

But the blow in the stomach had been too heavy and it was clear that Do Escobar's nervous system had suffered. One could see that he could no longer double his fists properly in order to land his blows, and his eyes had an expression as though he were not quite conscious. But as he felt that his muscles were giving way, he began, out of sheer vanity, to conduct himself as follows: he began to play the temperamental Latin, who was bent upon teasing the German bear by his nimbleness and thus driving him to desperation. He began to cavort all around Jappe in a small circle, taking short steps and making all kinds of superfluous movements, and then he attempted to laugh in an arrogant manner, which, considering his weakened condition, did not fail to make a heroic impression upon me. But Jappe did not grow at all desperate; he simply kept turning on his heel and delivering many a good blow, at the same time with his left arm fending off Do Escobar's feeble and trifling attacks. What sealed Do Escobar's fate, however, was the circumstance that his trousers kept constantly slipping down, so that even his striped under-shirt began to creep out and up, revealing a strip of his bare, yellowish body, which caused some to laugh. Why had he taken off his braces? He should not have paid any attention to considerations of mere looks. For now his trousers incommoded him, had in fact incommoded him during the entire fight. He was always trying to tighten them, and to thrust his little under-shirt inside them, for in spite of his evil state he could not bear the thought that he offered a deranged and comic spectacle. And so it happened, as he was still fighting with only one hand and trying to improve his toilet with the other, that Jappe gave him such a blow on the nose that I am still unable to understand to this day why it was not completely demolished.

The blood gushed forth and Do Escobar turned

aside, trying to stop the blood with his right hand, and with his left he made a most eloquent gesture behind his back. Jappe still stood, his knock-kneed legs apart and with fists held in position, and waited for Do Escobar to come on again. But Do Escobar had had enough. If I understood him correctly, he was the more respectable of the two and had come to the opinion that it was high time to put an end to the game. Jappe, no doubt, would have continued to fight even with a bloody nose, but almost as surely Do Escobar would have refused his co-operation in this case, and so he did this all the more resolutely since it was he himself who was bleeding. His nose had been made to bleed — the devil! — things ought never to have gone as far as that, he thought! The blood ran down between his fingers upon his clothes, defiled his light-coloured trousers, and dripped upon his light-tan boots. This was simple beastliness, nothing else, and in such circumstances he simply refused to fight any longer, for that would have been inhuman.

And besides, his view of the situation was that of the majority. Herr Knaak came into the circle and declared the fight over. " Honour has been amply satisfied," said he. " Both have put up a good fight." One could see how greatly relieved he was that the affair had gone off so smoothly.

" But there was no knock-out! " cried Johnny, astonished and disillusioned.

Jappe was also quite content to regard the case as settled and went towards his clothes, drawing a deep breath. Herr Knaak's fragile fiction that the match had remained undecided was unanimously accepted. Jappe was congratulated, but only on the sly; others lent their handkerchiefs to Do Escobar, as his own was soon saturated with blood. " Next! " was now the cry. " Now we must have another match! "

This voiced the wish of the entire crowd. The fight between Jappe and Do Escobar had been too brief, a mere ten minutes, hardly longer. All were on hand, there was plenty of time, something ought to be undertaken! So on with the next match and let him who wished to prove that he was a real fellow enter the arena in his turn.

No one applied. But why did my heart begin to beat like a little kettledrum at this summons? What I had feared had come to pass; demands were being made upon the spectators. But why did it seem to me now almost as though I had been looking forward with a kind of terrified joy to this supreme moment; and why was I, as soon as it had come, plunged into a whirl of antagonistic emotions? I looked at Johnny; he sat there beside me in perfect serenity, without the slightest participation, turned the straw in his mouth, and looked round him with an open and curious mien, to see whether another pair of strong bullies could not be found willing to let their noses be smashed for his own private enjoyment. How did it happen that I should find this challenge directed personally at me and, in the midst of my terrible excitement, feel myself in honour pledged to overcome my shyness by some tremendous, almost dreamlike effort and to attract the attention of all to myself by entering the lists as a hero? As a matter of fact, whether from vanity or excessive shyness, I was about to raise my hand and report myself for battle when an impudent voice, somewhere from out the crowd, was heard to cry: " Now Herr Knaak ought to fight! "

All eyes were sharply turned upon Herr Knaak. Was I not right in saying that he had ventured upon dangerous ground, that he was in peril of being forced to undergo an ordeal, a test of heart, lights, and liver? But he merely replied: " Oh, thanks! I got enough lickings when I was a boy! " He was saved. With eel-like glibness he had manœuvred himself out of the snare, had hinted at his years, had given them to understand that he had not evaded an honest fight in earlier days, and in doing this he had not even boasted, but had lent his words the very cast of truth, by confessing in sympathetic mockery of himself that he had been thrashed. And so he was left alone. One could see that it would be difficult, if not impossible, to get the best of him.

" Well, then, let's have a wrestling-match! " someone demanded. This proposal met with little favour. But in the very midst of the discussion following this suggestion Do Escobar (and I shall never forget the painful impression this made) let his hoarse Spanish voice be heard from behind his reddened handkerchief: " Wrestling is cowardly. Germans love to wrestle! "

This was an unheard-of bit of tactlessness on his part, and it was punished forthwith as it deserved to be. For Herr Knaak at once gave him this excellent answer: " Possibly. But it also seems that Germans are able at times to give Spaniards a good thrashing."

A burst of approving laughter rewarded him; his position was greatly fortified after this encounter, and Do Escobar was finished for good that day.

And yet it was the general impression that wrestling really was more or less tiresome and so one took to killing time with all sorts of acrobatic feats — with playing leap-frog, standing on one's head, walking on one's hands, and the like.

" Come on, we'll go now," said Johnny to

Brattström and me and stood up. That was just like Johnny Bishop. He had come here because something real with a sanguinary conclusion was to be offered him. But when the affair turned into mere play, he went away.

It was through him that I received my first impressions of the peculiar superiority of the national character of the English, which later on I learned so greatly to admire.

1911

THE INFANT PRODIGY

THE INFANT PRODIGY

THE infant prodigy enters — the entire hall grows silent.

It grows silent, and then the people begin to clap, because somewhere a born ruler of men and leader of the herd has started the applause. They have as yet heard nothing, but they clap their hands, for a mighty advertising campaign has paved the way for the infant prodigy, and the people are already under a spell, whether they are aware of it or not.

The infant prodigy emerges from behind a magnificent screen, which is embroidered all over with garlands in the Empire style and large, fabulous flowers. He hurriedly climbs the steps to the platform and walks into the applause, as into a bath, shivering a bit, touched by a slight shudder, and yet as into a friendly element. The boy goes to the edge of the platform, smiles as though he were about to be photographed, and thanks the audience with a small, shy, charming, and very girlish bow.

He is dressed entirely in white silk, which does not

fail of its effect upon the audience. He wears a small white silk jacket of fantastic cut, with a sash beneath it, and even his shoes are of white silk. But the bare legs contrast sharply with the white silk knickers, for they are quite brown; the boy is a Greek.

His name is Bibi Saccellaphylaccas. This is really his name. No one knows of what Christian name "Bibi" may be an abbreviation or pet form, none save the impresario, and he regards it as a business secret. Bibi's hair is smooth and black and hangs down to his shoulders. Yet it is parted sideways and held back from the small, brown, bulging forehead by means of a small silk bow. He has the most innocent, childlike face in the world, with an unformed little nose and an unsophisticated mouth; only that part of his face which lies below the coal-black, mouselike eyes is already a little weary and clearly expressive of two traits of character. He looks as though he were nine years old, but he is only eight as yet and is announced as only seven. People do not know themselves whether they really believe this. Perhaps they know better and nevertheless believe it, as they are so often wont to do. A bit of falsehood, they think, belongs to beauty. What, they think, would become of recreation and edification after the day's work if they did not come with a bit of goodwill, and let two and two make five? And they are quite right, with that collective mind of theirs!

The infant prodigy bows until the rustle of greetings has laid itself; then he goes to the grand piano, and the people throw a final glance at the program. The first number is " *Marche solennelle*," then " *Rêverie*," and then " *Le Hibou et les moineaux* " — all by Bibi Saccellaphylaccas. The entire program is by him — these are his own compositions. He cannot, to be sure, write them down, but he has them all safe in his small, uncommon head, and they must be accorded artistic significance, as the posters prepared by the impresario attest in a sober, matter-of-fact style. It appears that the impresario has wrested this concession from his critical nature in severe struggles.

The infant prodigy sits down upon the revolving stool and angles for the pedals with his little legs. These pedals are raised much higher than usual by means of an ingenious contrivance, so that Bibi may reach them. The grand piano is his own and he takes it everywhere with him. It rests upon wooden blocks, and its polish is rather damaged by its being transported so frequently, but all that merely makes the thing more interesting.

Bibi puts his silky white feet upon the pedals; the expression of his little face grows pointed and arch;

103

he looks straight before him and raises his right hand. It is a naïve, brown, childish little hand, but the wrist is strong and not at all childish, for it reveals well-developed joints.

Bibi puts on this mien for his audience, for he knows that he must entertain it a little. But he himself, for his part, takes a quiet pleasure in the affair, a pleasure that he could not describe to anyone. It is this nervous joy, this secret thrill of bliss, which creeps through him whenever he sits down in front of the open piano — and he will never lose this feeling. Again the keys offer themselves to his fingers, these seven black and white octaves, amongst which he has so often lost himself in adventures and profoundly exciting experiences and which nevertheless appear again as pure and untouched as a drawing-slate that has been wiped off. It is music, the world of music, that lies before him! It lies outspread before him like a tempting sea and he is able to plunge in and swim about blissfully, allow himself to be borne hither and thither, let himself go down in a storm and yet keep the mastery in his hands, govern and dispose of it all. — He holds his right hand aloft.

There is a breathless stillness in the hall. It is this tension before the first chord — how will it begin? It begins thus: Bibi fetches the first tone out of the piano with his forefinger, an unexpectedly powerful tone in the middle register, resembling a trumpet-blast. Others align themselves to this, and the introduction begins — the muscles of the audience relax.

The hall is a very ornate one, situated in a first-class fashionable hotel, with paintings showing much rosy flesh upon the walls, with luxuriant pillars, mirrors with heavily decorated frames, and a vast number, a perfect solar system, of electric bulbs, which sprout forth everywhere in clusters and fill the room with a thin, golden, celestial radiance, far brighter than day. — No chair is empty; yes, people are standing even in the side aisles and at the back of the hall. In front, where the price is twelve marks (for the impresario is devoted to the principle of awe-inspiring prices), we find the members of high society; for there is a lively interest in the infant prodigy in these lofty circles. Many uniforms are visible and a great deal of good taste in the matter of evening toilets. — There are even a number of children there, who let their legs dangle in a well-bred manner from their chairs and who regard their small, gifted, and silky white colleague with shining eyes.

In front to the left sits the mother of the infant prodigy, a very corpulent dame, with a powdered double chin, and a plume in her hair, and at her side is the impresario, a gentleman of oriental type, with large golden buttons in his far-protruding cuffs. The princess is seated in the middle of the first row. She is a small, wrinkled, dried-up old princess, but she patronizes the arts, in so far as they are refined. She is seated in a deep fauteuil of plush, and Persian rugs are spread before her. She holds her hands folded upon her striped grey dress of silk, close beneath her breast, inclines her head to one side, and affords a picture of aristocratic peace, as she contemplates the infant prodigy in action. Her lady-in-waiting sits beside her, dressed in a costume of striped green silk. But she is for all that only a lady-in-waiting and must not even lean back in her chair.

Bibi comes to a close with a great flourish. With what force this urchin handles the piano! One can scarcely believe one's ears. The theme of the march, a swinging, enthusiastic melody, breaks forth once more in a passage of full harmony, broadly and boastfully, and at every chord Bibi throws back the upper part of his body, as though he were marching triumphantly in a festival procession. He then closes grandly, slips in a crouching attitude sidewise from his stool, and waits smiling for the applause.

And the applause bursts forth, unanimous, touched, enraptured. Just see the dainty hips of the child, as he makes his girlish bow! Clap! Clap! Wait, I'll take off my gloves! Bravo, little Saccophylax, or whatever your name may be! Why, he is a perfect little devil of a fellow!

Bibi must come forth thrice from behind the screen before the people are satisfied. A few stragglers, tardy arrivals, come crowding in from behind and find place with great difficulty in this full hall. And then the concert proceeds.

Bibi lets his " *Rêverie* " flow liquidly — it is entirely composed of arpeggios, over which from time to time a bit of melody lifts itself with feeble wings; and then he plays " *Le Hibou et les moineaux.*" This piece is a great success, and exerts a stirring effect upon the audience. It is a real child's piece and marvellously fanciful. The bass notes show us the owl sitting and dolefully opening and shutting his veiled eyes; then in the treble the sparrows flutter, pertly yet timorously, as they tease him. Four times Bibi is called out with jubilation after this piece. An employé of the hotel in a brass-buttoned livery carries three huge wreaths of laurel up to the platform, and holds them in front of him, from the side, while Bibi bows his thanks. Even the princess participates in the applause, by gently touching her flat hands against each other, even though no sound ensues.

How well this small, accomplished wight knows how to draw out the applause! He keeps them waiting from his place behind the screen, lingers a little upon the steps of the platform, regards the coloured satin bows of the wreaths with childish pleasure, even though they have long since begun to bore him, bows charmingly and hesitatingly, and leaves the people time to work off their enthusiasm, so that none of the precious noise of their palms is lost. " ' *Le Hibou* ' is my strong card," he thinks, for he has learned this term from the impresario. " Then comes the ' *Fantaisie,*' which is really much better, especially the place in C sharp. But you have gone mad about this *hibou,* you public, although it is the first thing and the stupidest which I have ever made." And he bows graciously.

He then plays a " *Méditation* " and then an " *Étude* " — it is a most comprehensive program. The " *Méditation* " goes much like the " *Rêverie,*" which is no reflection upon it, and in the " *Étude* " Bibi shows all his technical dexterity, which is slightly inferior to his power of invention. And then comes the " *Fantaisie.*" It is his favourite piece. He always plays it a bit differently, treats it in a free manner, and at times surprises himself by new turns and conceits, when he is in good form.

He sits and plays, very small and shining white in front of the great black piano, lone and elect upon the platform over that blurred mass of humanity, which has only one heavy soul, to be moved with difficulty, a soul upon which he must operate with his own, lone and lifted above the multitude. — His soft black hair, together with the white silk bow, has fallen across his forehead; his strong, bony, trained wrists are in action, and one sees the muscles of his brown, childish cheeks strain and quiver.

At times there come to him seconds of forgetfulness and solitude, during which his strange, mouselike eyes, with their dull circles, glide sideways from the audience towards the frescoed wall of the hall at his side, through which they peer, in order to lose themselves in adventurous distances filled with a vague life. And then a glance from the corners of his eyes darts back into the hall and he is again one with his hearers.

" Complaint and jubilation, a soaring aloft and a profound plunge — my *'Fantaisie'!* " thinks Bibi, quite tenderly. " Now listen, here comes the part which goes into C sharp! " And he lets the pedals play, as it goes into C sharp. Are they aware of it? In faith, not in the least, they are aware of nothing! And so he casts his eyes up prettily towards the ceiling, so that they may at least have something to look at.

The people sit there in long rows and look at the infant prodigy. And they think all manner of thoughts with their collective brain. An old gentleman with a white beard, a seal-ring on his forefinger, and a knotty growth on his bald pate, an excrescence, if you will, thinks to himself: " One ought really to be ashamed of oneself. One has never been able to get beyond playing ' Three Hunters from the Palatinate,' and here one sits as an old greybeard and has miracles performed for one by this midget. But one must not forget that this gift is a divine one. God bestows his gifts as He will; there is no help for that, and it is no shame to be an ordinary human being. It is somewhat as with the child Jesus. One may bow before a child without being ashamed. How comforting to feel this! " He does not dare to think: " How sweet it is! " " Sweet " would be unworthy of a robust old gentleman. But he feels it! He feels it for all that!

" Art — " thinks the business man with the parrot-like nose. " Of course! Art brings a bit of a gleam into life, a little tinkle, a touch of white silk. And the deal furthermore is not a bad one. There are at least fifty seats at twelve marks apiece sold; that alone makes six hundred marks — and then all the incidentals.

110

Deducting the rent of the hall, and the cost of lighting and the programs, there will be a balance of at least a thousand marks. Not at all to be despised."

" Well, that was Chopin that he just played," thinks the piano-teacher, a lady with a pointed nose, of about that age when hopes begin to go to sleep and the intelligence acquires an additional sharpness. " One might say that the boy is not very direct. I shall say afterwards that he is not very direct. That sounds well. The way he holds his hands is, moreover, very undisciplined. One should be able to lay a coin upon the back of the hand — I should give him a bit of the ruler."

A young girl, who looks very waxen-faced, and who is of an age in which there are certain tensions inducing delicious thoughts, thinks to herself: " What is it that he is playing there? Why, it is passion, passion, that he is playing! But he is a mere child! Were he to kiss me, it would seem as though my little brother kissed me — it would not be a kiss at all. Can it be that there is a passion that is disconnected from all earthy things, pure passion, something that is only passionate child's-play? — Well, if I should say that aloud, they would dose me with cod-liver oil. That is the way of the world."

An officer leans against a pillar. He surveys the

successful Bibi and thinks: " You are somebody and I am somebody, each in his own way." He draws his heels together and pays the infant prodigy that homage which he pays to all existent powers.

The critic, however, an ageing man in a seedy black coat and turned-up, mud-spattered trousers, occupies his free seat, and thinks: " Just look at this Bibi, this urchin! As an individual he has still some distance to go, but as a type he is quite finished — it is the type of the artist. He carries in him the majesty of the artist as well as his lack of dignity, his charlatanism and his sacred spark, his contempt and his secret rapture. But I must not write that — it is really too good. Ah, yes, believe me, I might have become an artist myself if I had not seen through it all so clearly."

The infant prodigy has finished and a veritable tempest of applause breaks loose. He is forced to appear again and again from behind his screen. The man with the brass buttons comes with new garlands in tow, four laurel wreaths, a lyre made of violets, a bouquet of roses. His two arms do not suffice to hand all these tributes to the infant prodigy; the impresario himself ascends the platform to help him. He hangs a laurel wreath round Bibi's neck; he strokes his black hair tenderly. And suddenly, as though he were overcome by emotion, he bends low and bestows a kiss upon the infant prodigy, a sounding kiss, full upon the mouth. This causes the tempest to increase to a hurricane. This kiss acts like a galvanic shock upon the audience; it shoots through the crowd and thrills every nerve. The people are borne away by a mad desire for noise. Loud bravos mingle with the wild tumult of hands. Several of Bibi's small and matter-of-fact comrades down there wave their handkerchiefs. — But the critic thinks: " Of course, that kiss from the impresario was bound to come. An old and effective trick. Yes, by heavens! if one only didn't see through it all so plainly! "

And then the concert of the infant prodigy draws to a close. It began at half past seven and is over by half past eight. The platform is filled with garlands, and two small flower-pots are standing upon the lamp-brackets of the grand piano. Bibi plays his " *Rhapsodie grecque* " as his final number and this passes at the close into the Greek national hymn. Those of Bibi's countrymen who happen to be present would like to join in and sing this, if this concert were not such a fashionable one. They compensate themselves at the close by making a tremendous noise, a hot-blooded row, a national demonstration. But the ageing critic thinks: " Of course, that national hymn was

113

bound to come. One plays the whole affair into another sphere, no means of rousing enthusiasm is left
untried. I'll write that such things are inartistic. But
perhaps it is artistic after all. What is the artist? A
clown. Criticism is the highest of all functions. But I
cannot write that." And then he removes himself with
his bespattered trousers.

After nine or ten calls the overheated infant prodigy
no longer retires behind his screen, but goes down to
his mamma and to the impresario in the hall. The
people are standing among the disarranged chairs and
applauding and pushing forwards in order to have a
look at Bibi close at hand. A few also wish to have a
look at the princess; two close-packed groups form in
front of the platform, around the infant prodigy and
the princess, and it is difficult to say which of the two
is really receiving. But then the lady-in-waiting is
commanded to go to Bibi; she tugs and smoothes his
silken jacket a bit, to make him presentable for court,
leads him by the arm in front of the princess, and earnestly indicates to him that he should kiss the hand of
Her Royal Highness.

" How do you do it, my child? " asks the princess.
" Does it come to you by itself, when you sit down? "

" *Oui, madame*," Bibi replies. But inwardly he
thinks: " Oh, you stupid old princess — ! "

Then he turns away with a shy rudeness and goes back to his own people.

Outside there is great confusion at the cloak-rooms. One holds up one's check; with open arms one receives furs, shawls, and galoshes across the table. The piano-teacher is standing there among her acquaintances and criticizing. " He is not very direct," says she aloud, and looks about her.

A young, aristocratic lady is standing in front of one of the tall mirrors against the wall, and her two brothers, both lieutenants, are helping her with her cloak and her fur overshoes. She is wonderfully pretty, with her steel-blue eyes and her clear, thorough-bred face, a perfect little aristocrat. Done with her dressing, she stands waiting for her brothers.

" Adolf, don't stand in front of the mirror so long! " she says to one of them in a low, angry voice, for he finds it difficult to tear himself away from the image of his handsome but fatuous face. Well, if that does not beat everything! Surely Lieutenant Adolf has the right to button his overcoat in front of a mirror without her leave! Then they go out, and outside in the street, where the arc-lamps shimmer turbidly through the whirling snow, Lieutenant Adolf begins to cut up a bit — turns up his coat-collar, shoves his hands into the slanting pockets of his overcoat, and begins to execute a short cakewalk upon the snow, for it is very cold.

"A child!" thinks a girl with unkempt hair who walks with dangling arms behind them, in the company of a solemn-looking youth. "A most lovable child! In there everything was full of reverence —" Then with a loud, monotonous voice she says: "We are all infant prodigies, we creators!"

"Well," thinks the old gentleman who has never been able to get beyond "Three Huntsmen from the Palatinate," and whose excrescence is now covered by a top hat, "what does she mean? A kind of Pythia, it seems to me."

But the solemn-looking youth, who understands her every word, nods slowly.

Then they are silent and the girl with unkempt hair follows that aristocratic sister and her brothers with her eyes. She despises them, yet she follows them with her eyes, until they have vanished round the corner.

1903

TOBIAS MINDERNICKEL

TOBIAS MINDERNICKEL

~~~~~~~~~~~~~

ONE of the streets which run rather steeply from Quay
Alley up to the centre of the city is called the Grey
Way. About the middle of this street, on the right
hand as you come from the river, stands a house
labelled No. 47, a narrow drab-coloured structure, in
no way distinguished from its neighbours. There is a
small shop on the ground-floor, in which one can buy
rubber overshoes and cod-liver oil. On entering the
hallway, which gives upon a courtyard in which cats
are prowling about, one sees a narrow and worn
wooden staircase, saturated with the inexpressible
musty smells of poverty, leading to the upper stories.
A carpenter lives on the left side of the first story, a
midwife on the right. The second story harbours a cob-
bler on the left, and on the right a lady who begins to
sing loudly as soon as steps are heard on the staircase. The flat on the third story to the left is empty;
the one to the right is occupied by a man by the name
of Mindernickel, who also bears the name of Tobias.
There is a story about this man which must be told,

because it is full of riddles, and shameful beyond belief.

The externals of Mindernickel are remarkable, odd, and ridiculous. For instance, one sees him when he takes a walk, supporting his lean figure on a cane as he proceeds along the street, always clothed in black, from head to foot. He wears an old-fashioned, bell-topped, rough tall hat, a tight-fitting frock-coat shiny with age, and equally shabby trousers, which are frayed out at the bottom and far too short, so that one sees the gores of his gaiters. It must, however, be said that these clothes of his are brushed in the most scrupulous manner. His lean neck appears the longer because it lifts itself from a low folding collar. His grey hair is combed back smoothly over the temples, and the broad brim of the tall hat shades a pale, smooth-shaven face with sunken cheeks, with inflamed eyes, which are seldom raised from the ground, and two deep furrows which run sorrowfully from the nostrils to the down-drawn corners of the mouth.

Mindernickel seldom goes forth, and there is a reason for this. As soon as he appears on the street, a great many children gather, follow him for quite a distance, laughing, mocking, and singing: " Ho, ho, Tobias! " and even pull him by the coat-tails, while the people come to the doors and enjoy the spectacle. He himself, however, goes on without defending himself, looking shyly about him, with high-drawn shoulders and extended head, like a man who hurries through a shower without an umbrella; and even though people laugh in his face, he greets with a humble politeness this or that person standing before their doors. Later, when the children remain behind, when he comes to parts where he is not known, and only a few turn to look at him, his behaviour does not greatly alter. He continues to peer about him anxiously and to hurry along in a hang-dog manner, as though he felt a thousand mocking glances levelled at him, and when he lifts his eyes, shyly and irresolutely, then one observes the strange fact that he is unable to look any person straight and quietly in the eyes, or even regard an object with fixity. He appears to lack, however strangely this may sound, the natural superiority of the sense of perception with which a human being looks upon the world of phenomena about him; he appears to feel himself inferior to every phenomenon, and his uneasy eyes must seek the ground in the face of men and of things.

What are the circumstances attending this man, who is always alone and who appears to be unhappy in an uncommon degree? His forced middle-class dress, as

121

well as a certain careful motion of the hand across the chin, seems to indicate that he does not in any circumstances wish to be reckoned as belonging to that class of population amid which he is living. God knows what tricks Fate has played upon him. He looks as though Life had laughed contemptuously as it gave him a blow full in the face. It is also possible that he has not suffered any great disasters at the hands of destiny and is simply not fitted to cope with it. The painful inferiority and idiotic aspect of his appearance give one the painful impression that nature has refused him the necessary measure of balance, power, and backbone which would enable him to exist with head erect.

After he has taken a walk, supported by his black cane, into town, he is wont to return to his home by the Grey Way, where the children receive him with jeers. He walks up the musty steps to his rooms, which are bare and poor. Only the bureau, an excellent piece of Empire furniture, with heavy metal handles, is fine and valuable. In front of the window, the view from which is hopelessly cut off by the tall side-wall of the neighbouring house, stands a flower-pot full of earth. Though nothing grows in this pot, Tobias Minder-nickel occasionally goes up to it, regards it earnestly, and smells the bare soil within it. Adjacent to this

122

room there is a small, dark bedroom. After he has entered, Tobias puts his tall hat and his cane upon the table, sits down on the green-covered sofa, which smells of dust, supports his chin in his hand, and looks with raised eyebrows at the floor. It seems that there is really nothing else on earth left for him to do.

As to Mindernickel's character, it is very difficult to judge of this; the following incident seems to speak in his favour. One day as this singular man left the house, and as usual a swarm of children gathered and followed him with mocking cries and laughter, a boy of some ten years stumbled over the foot of another and pitched so heavily upon the pavement that the blood ran from his nose and forehead and he lay where he fell, crying. Tobias thereupon turned round, hurried up to the prostrate lad, bent over him, and began to express his compassion in a mild and trembling voice.

"You poor child," said he, "did you hurt yourself? You are bleeding! See, the blood is running down his forehead! Oh, how sad to see you lying there that way! Of course it hurts him — that's why the poor little fellow is crying. Oh, I'm so sorry! It was your fault, but I'll tie my handkerchief about your head. So, so! Now be brave, now come and get on your feet again!"

123

After he had spoken these words and tied his own handkerchief about the boy's head, he raised him carefully to his feet and went on his way. His attitude and his face were, however, at this moment quite different from what they usually were. He walked upright and with a firm tread, and his chest expanded with deep breaths under the tight frock-coat; his eyes had grown larger, had become bright, and looked with assurance upon the world of men and things, while a trace of painful happiness lingered about his lips.

This incident had the effect for a time of somewhat diminishing the delight which the denizens of the Grey Way took in mockery. But after some time had elapsed, his surprising action was forgotten, and a great number of healthy, cheery, and cruel throats once more shouted after the stooped and indecisive man: " Ho, ho, Tobias! "

ONE sunny forenoon at eleven o'clock Mindernickel left the house and walked through the entire town out towards the Lerchenberg, a far-stretching hill, which constituted the most fashionable afternoon promenade of the place. The pleasant spring weather which prevailed at this time had, however, induced a number of pedestrians and owners of carriages to visit the promenade thus early. A man with a young hunting-dog on a leash stood under one of the trees in the avenue, and manifested to the passers-by his intention of selling this dog. It was a small, yellow, and muscular animal, about four months old, with a black ring about one eye, and one black ear.

As Tobias noticed this at a distance of ten paces, he stood still, passed his hand across his chin several times, and looked thoughtfully at the man and the little dog with its tail wagging alertly. He then went on again, and, with the crook of his cane pressed against his mouth, thrice encircled the tree against which the man was leaning, then went up to him, and, while he kept his eye fixed upon the dog, asked in a low and hasty voice: " How much for the dog? "

" Ten marks," said the man.

Tobias was silent for a moment and then repeated, indecisively: " Ten marks? "

" Yes," said the man.

Tobias then drew forth a black leather purse from his pocket, took out a five-mark, a three- and a two-mark note, hastily handed this money to the seller of the dog, seized the leash, and with a shy and humble glance about him — for a number of people had observed the sale and were laughing — pulled the yelping and struggling animal along behind him. He fought the entire way, braced his forelegs against the ground, and looked up with anxious, questioning eye at his new master, who kept on tugging with silent energy, and so they came safely back through the town.

A vast commotion ensued among the street children of the Grey Way when Tobias appeared with the dog, but he took him in his arms, bent his head over him, and hurried through the mocking cries and the laughter, and the pulls at his coat-tails, up the stairs and into his room. Here he put down the dog, who was persistently whining, stroked him kindly, and said with condescension: " Well, well, you needn't be afraid of me, you animal; that's quite unnecessary."

Hereupon he opened a drawer in the bureau and took out a plate with cooked meat and potatoes, and threw a portion of this to the dog, which at once stopped whining and swallowed the food with smacking chops and wagging tail.

" And your name is going to be Esau," said Tobias; " do you understand? Esau. You will be able to remember that simple sound." Then, pointing at the floor in front of him, he called in a tone of command: " Esau! "

The dog, no doubt in hopes of getting still more to eat, came at the call. Tobias patted his sides approvingly, and said: " Quite right, my friend; you deserve praise."

He then stepped back a few paces, pointed at the floor again, and commanded anew: " Esau! "

And the animal, which had grown quite merry, again came bounding up and licked the boots of his master.

This trick Tobias repeated at least twelve or fourteen times, with unflagging pleasure in the command and its execution; but finally the dog appeared to be tired; he seemed anxious to rest and digest, and laid himself down upon the floor in the pretty and clever pose which hunting-dogs assume, with both of his long and delicately shaped forelegs stretched out close beside each other.

" Once more! " said Tobias. " Esau! "

But Esau turned his head aside and did not move.

" Esau! " cried Tobias, with loud, imperious voice, " you've got to come, even when you're tired! "

But Esau laid his head upon his paws and did not come.

" See here! " said Tobias, and his voice was full of suppressed and terrible threats, " you obey, or you'll discover that it's not wise to irritate me! "

But the dog merely moved his tail a little. Hereupon Mindernickel was seized by a vast, a disproportionate and furious anger. He seized his black cane, lifted Esau by the scruff of his neck, and began to rain blows upon the yelping little animal. Beside himself with furious indignation, he kept repeating in a terribly hissing voice: " So! you disobey? You dare to disobey me? "

Finally he threw the stick aside, put the whimpering dog on the floor, and began walking up and down with his hands behind his back, drawing deep breaths, while now and again he threw a disdainful and angry glance at Esau. After he had paced to and fro for a time, he stood still before the animal, which lay upon its back and moved its front legs in a beseeching fashion. Tobias folded his arms upon his breast and spoke with that dreadfully cold, hard look and voice with which Napoleon confronted the company which had lost its eagle in battle: " How have you behaved yourself, if I may ask? "

And the dog, already happy at this advance, crawled still closer, snuggled against the leg of his master, and looked up at him imploringly with his shining eyes.

For quite a while Tobias looked down upon the humiliated creature in silence, but then, as he began to feel the tender warmth of the body against his leg, he took Esau in his arms.

128

"Well, I will have pity on you," he said; then, as the affectionate animal began to lick his face, his mood was suddenly changed to tenderness and sadness. He pressed the dog to his breast in a burst of poignant affection, his eyes filled with tears, and without finishing his exclamation he kept on repeating with suffocated voice: "See, you are my only one — my only one — " He then put Esau carefully upon the sofa, sat down beside him, and, chin in hand, regarded him with a mild and peaceful look.

Tobias Mindernickel now left the house still less frequently than before, for he felt no inclination to show himself publicly with Esau. He devoted his whole attention to the dog; yes, he occupied himself from morning till evening with nothing else than feeding him, wiping his eyes, ordering him about, scolding him, and talking with him in a most human manner. It was a fact, however, that Esau did not always conduct himself to his owner's satisfaction. When Esau lay beside him on the sofa and, sleepy for lack of fresh air and exercise, looked at him with melancholy eyes, then Tobias was full of contentment; he sat there quietly in an attitude of great self-satisfaction and stroked Esau's back in pity, while he remarked: "You are looking at me with a very pained

129

expression, my poor friend? Yes, yes, the world is a sad place, you too have discovered that, young as you are! "

But when the animal, blind and wild with the instinct of play and the chase, raced about the room, tugged and tussled with an old felt slipper, sprang upon the chairs, and tumbled about in his exceeding joy, Tobias would then follow these doings from a distance with a puzzled, disapproving, and uncertain look and a smile that was sinister and full of vexation, until he would finally call the dog in a harsh tone and shout at him: " Stop that silliness! There is no reason for gambolling."

It even happened one day that Esau escaped from the room, and raced down the steps to the street, where he began to chase a cat, to mouth the street manure, and, quite beside himself, to play about with the children. Then as Tobias appeared with painfully distorted features and was greeted by the applause and laughter of half the street, the sad thing occurred — the dog bounded away from his master in long leaps. On that day Tobias thrashed him for a long time and with great bitterness.

One day — the dog had now been his property for several weeks — Tobias took a loaf of bread from the drawer of the bureau to feed Esau, and began

130

to cut off small bits with the large, bone-handled knife which he was accustomed to use for this purpose; these bits he let fall upon the floor. The dog, however, carried away by hunger and silliness, leaped blindly into the air, ran the knife, which was clumsily held, into his right shoulder-blade, and then lay bleeding and twisting on the floor.

Tobias, appalled, threw everything aside and bent over the wounded creature. Then suddenly the expression of his features changed, and it is a fact that a gleam of relief and happiness lighted up his face. Carefully he carried the whimpering dog to the sofa, and it is difficult to describe with what devotion he began to tend the sick animal. He would not leave his side the whole day long; at night he let him sleep on his own bed; he washed and bandaged him, patted, comforted, and pitied him with indefatigable joy and solicitude.

" Does it hurt very much? " he would ask. " Yes, yes, my poor fellow, I know you suffer sorely. But never mind, we must bear it." His face, as he spoke these words, was peaceful, sad, and yet content.

In that degree, however, in which Esau recovered his strength and became convalescent, the behaviour of Tobias became more restless and discontented. He

131

now considered it right not to trouble himself any more about the wound, but merely to show his pity for the dog by words or by petting him. But the wound was pretty well cured; Esau's constitution was excellent, and he soon began to run about the room once more, and one day, after he had lapped up a plate of milk and white bread, he leaped from the sofa completely cured, and went charging about the two rooms with joyous yappings and all the old abandon, to tug at the bed-spread, to chase a potato to and fro, and to turn somersaults out of sheer fun.

Tobias stood at the window, near the flower-pot, and while one of his hands, protruding lean and skinny from his frayed sleeves, fumbled mechanically at the hair which he had stroked far back from his temples, his figure stood outlined strange and black against the grey wall of the neighbouring house. His face was pale and distorted by grief, as he immovably followed Esau's boundings with a squinting, embarrassed, envious, and sinister look. Suddenly, however, he pulled himself together, went towards him, caught him, and lifted him slowly in his arms.

" My poor fellow! " he began in a pathetic tone — but Esau, full of playfulness and not at all disposed to let himself be treated still further in this manner,

132

snapped sportively at the hand that wished to stroke him, writhed out of the arms that held him, sprang to the floor, made a mischievous side-jump, yapped, and ran away gaily.

What now happened was something so inexplicable and infamous that I simply refuse to relate it in detail. Tobias Mindernickel stood there, leaning forward a little, with his arms hanging down at his sides. His lips were pressed together and his eyeballs trembled eerily in their sockets. And then, suddenly, with a kind of insane leap, he had seized the animal, a long, shining object flashed in his hand, and the dog, with a deep cut from the right shoulder to the chest, fell to the floor. He did not utter a sound, he simply fell upon his side, bleeding and panting.

The next moment he lay upon the sofa, and Tobias was kneeling in front of him, pressing a cloth upon the wound, and stammering: " My poor fellow! My poor, dear doggy! How sad everything is! How sad both of us are! Do you suffer? Yes, yes, I know you suffer — how miserably you lie there before me! But I am with you, I am here beside you. I'll comfort you! I'll get my best handkerchief — "

But Esau lay there with a rattling in his throat. His dulled and questioning eyes, full of a lack of

133

understanding, innocence, and accusation, were directed upon his master — and then he stretched out his legs a little and died.

Tobias remained motionless. He had laid his face upon Esau's body and was weeping bitterly.

1897

THE PATH
TO THE CEMETERY

THE PATH TO THE CEMETERY

THE path to the cemetery ran always parallel to the highway, always side by side, until it had reached its goal; that is to say, the cemetery. On the other side there were human habitations, new structures of the suburbs, part of which were still in process of completion, and then came fields. As to the highway itself, this was flanked by trees, by knotty beeches of a good old age, and the road was half paved and half bare earth. But the path to the cemetery was thinly strewn with pebbles, which gave it the character of an agreeable foot-path. A small, dry ditch, filled with grass and wildflowers, extended between the two.

It was spring, and almost summer already. The whole world smiled. God's blue skies were covered with masses of small, round, compact little clouds, dotted with many snow-white little clumps which had an almost humorous look. The birds twittered in the beeches, and a mild wind swept across the fields.

A wagon from the neighbouring village crept towards the city; it rolled partly upon the paved, partly upon the unpaved part of the highway. The driver let his legs dangle on both sides of the shaft and whistled execrably. In the back part of the wagon there sat a little yellow dog with its back to him, and along its pointed little nose looked back with an unutterably grave and collected mien at the way it had just come. It was an incomparable, a most diverting little dog, worth its weight in gold; but it plays no part in this affair and so we must turn our faces from it. — A detachment of soldiers went marching by. They came from the garrison near by, marched in their own dust, and sang. A second wagon crept from the direction of the city towards the next village. The driver slept, and there was no little dog, for which reason this vehicle is entirely without interest. Two journeymen came striding along, the one hunch-backed, the other a giant in stature. They went barefooted, carrying their boots on their backs, called out cheerily to the sleeping driver, and strode on bravely. The traffic was moderate, regulating itself without complications or accidents.

The way to the cemetery was trodden by a solitary man; he walked slowly, with lowered head, and supported himself on a black stick. The man was called Piepsam, Lobgott (Praisegod) Piepsam and nothing else. We proclaim his name with a certain emphasis because subsequently he acted in a most peculiar manner.

He was dressed in black, for he was on the way to the graves of his loved ones. He wore a rough, cylindrical silk hat, a frock-coat shiny with age, trousers which were not only too narrow but also too short, and black kid gloves which were shabby all over. His throat, a long, lean throat with a large Adam's apple, lifted itself from a turnover collar which was frayed and displayed corners which had already become a little rough. But when the man raised his head, which he did at times in order to see how far he still was from the cemetery, then one was treated to a strange sight, a remarkable face, a face which beyond all question one was not likely soon to forget.

This face was smooth-shaven and pale. Between the hollowed-out cheeks there protruded a nose which thickened bulbously at the end, a nose which glowed with an irregular, unnatural red and which, quite superfluously, paraded a mass of little excrescences, unhealthy growths which gave it an unconventional and fantastic look. This nose, the dark rubicundity of which contrasted sharply with the dull pallor of the rest of the face, embodied something unreal and picturesque; it looked as though it were merely affixed like a masquerade nose, like a melancholy joke. But

139

it was not this alone. The man kept his mouth, a broad mouth with sunk corners, tightly closed, and whenever he looked up, he lifted his black eyebrows, which were shot through by little white hairs — lifted them beneath the brim of his hat, so that one might see how inflamed his eyes were and what dark circles surrounded them. In short, it was a face to which one could not permanently refuse the deepest sympathy.

Lobgott Piepsam's appearance was not a joyous one; it fitted in but badly with this charming forenoon, and it was even too dismal for one who was about to pay a visit to the graves of his loved ones. But looking into his heart and soul, one was forced to confess that there were sufficient grounds for all this. He was a trifle depressed? — it is difficult to convey this to people so merry as yourselves — perhaps a bit unhappy? — a trifle badly treated? Well, to tell the truth, he was all of these things not only a trifle, but to a high degree; he was, without any exaggeration, in a bad way.

First of all, he drank. But of this more anon. Furthermore he was a widower, had lost both parents, and stood abandoned by everybody; he had not a single soul to love him in all the world. His wife, whose maiden-name had been Lebzelt, had been reft from his side after she had borne him a child little less than half a year ago; it was the third child and it had been still-born. Both of the other children had also died — one of diphtheria, the other of really nothing at all — perhaps out of a general ineptitude. But this had not been enough, for soon after this he had lost his job, had been driven out of his petty position; and that bore a close relation to that passion of his which was mightier than Piepsam.

Formerly he had been able to resist it to some degree, although there were periods when he had been intemperately addicted to it. But after wife and children had been taken from him, after he had lost all his friends and stood alone in the world and without a single support or hold, his vice had mastered him and had broken his spiritual resistance more and more. He had been an official in the service of an insurance society, a kind of higher copyist with a monthly salary of ninety marks. While in his irresponsible condition, he had become guilty of gross negligence, and after having been repeatedly warned, he had been finally discharged as unreliable.

It is clear that this did not by any manner of means lead to a moral revolt on the part of Piepsam, but that he was thenceforth utterly doomed. For you must know that ill fortune slays the dignity of a man — it is just as well to have a little insight into these things.

141

There is a strange and dreadful concatenation of cause and effect here. There is no use in a man's protesting his own innocence; in most cases he will despise himself for his misfortune. But self-contempt and vice have a strange and horrible interrelationship; they feed each other, they play into each other's hands, in a way to make one's blood run cold. And that is the way it was with Piepsam. He drank because he did not respect himself, and he respected himself less and less because the continual shameful defeats of all his good resolutions devoured all his self-confidence. In a wardrobe in his home there usually stood a bottle containing a poisonous yellow fluid, a most pernicious fluid — we must be cautious and not mention its name. Lobgott Piepsam had literally knelt before this wardrobe and almost bitten his tongue in two; and in spite of this he would go down in defeat in the end. — We take no pleasure in relating these facts, but they are, after all, instructive.

And here he was walking along the path to the cemetery and prodding the ground with his black cane. A gentle wind played about his nose, but he did not feel it. His eyebrows elevated, he bent a hollow and turbid look upon the world about him — a lorn and miserable creature. — Suddenly he heard a noise behind him and pricked up his ears; a soft rushing sound was approaching with great rapidity from the distance. He turned about and stood still. — It was a bicycle, the tires of which crunched along the pebble-strewn path. It came on in full career, but then slackened its speed, for Piepsam stood in the middle of the way.

A young man sat in the saddle, a youth, a careless youth on a tour. He himself, great heavens, surely made no pretensions to belonging to the great and glorious ones of the world! He rode a machine of middling quality — it does not really matter of what make — a wheel costing, say, about two hundred marks. And with this he went pedalling a bit through the country, fresh from the city, riding with flashing pedals into God's green world — hurray! He wore a coloured shirt and a grey jacket, sports leggings, and the jauntiest little cap in the world — a very joke of a cap, with brown checks and a button on the top. And from under this cap a thick mop of blond hair welled forth and stood up above his forehead. His eyes were of a lightning-blue. He came on like Life itself and tinkled his bell, but Piepsam did not move a hair's breadth out of the way. He stood there and looked at Life with a rigid stare.

It looked angrily at him and rode slowly past him, whereupon Piepsam also began to walk on. But when it was ahead of him, he said slowly and with a weighty emphasis: " Number nine thousand seven hundred and seven."

He then pursed up his lips and stared incontinently at the ground, at the same time feeling that Life's eyes were bent upon him in perplexity.

It had turned round, had seized the saddle from behind with one hand, and rode very slowly.

" What? " it asked.

" Number nine thousand seven hundred and seven," repeated Piepsam. " Oh, nothing. I'll report you."

" You will report me? " Life asked, turned still further round, and rode still more slowly, so that it was obliged to wobble to and fro with the handle-bars.

" Certainly! " replied Piepsam at a distance of five or six steps.

" Why? " asked Life, and dismounted. It stood still and seemed full of expectancy.

" You know why well enough."

" No, I don't know why."

" You must know."

" But I do not know why," said Life, " and moreover I am not at all interested why." With this it was about to mount its wheel again. It was not at all at a loss for words.

144

" I will report you," said Piepsam, " because you ride here, on this path to the cemetery, and not out there on the high-road."

" But, my dear sir! " Life said, with an impatient and angry laugh, turned round once more, and stood still. " You see tracks of bicycles along the entire path. Everybody rides here."

" That's all one to me," retorted Piepsam; " I'll report you just the same."

" Well, do whatever you like! " Life cried, and mounted its wheel. It really mounted, it did not disgrace itself by making a mess of this; it gave a single thrust with its foot, sat securely on the saddle, and put forth all efforts to reacquire a speed in accordance with its temperament.

" If you keep on riding here, here on the path to the cemetery, I shall most surely report you! " cried Piepsam in a high and trembling voice. But Life really troubled itself very little about this; it rode off with increasing speed.

Had you seen Lobgott Piepsam's face at this moment, you would have been greatly frightened. He pressed his lips so firmly together that his cheeks and even the rubicund nose were twisted quite out of place, and his eyes, from beneath his unnaturally raised eyebrows, stared with an insane expression after the vehicle as it rolled away. Suddenly he dashed forwards. At a run he traversed the short distance which separated him from the machine, and seized the tool-case beneath the saddle. He held on to it with both hands, literally attached himself to it, and with lips still pressed together in an unnatural manner, dumb, and with wild eyes, he tugged with all his strength at the balancing bicycle as it speeded forwards. Anyone seeing him might well have doubted whether he intended, out of malice, to hinder the young man from riding on, or whether he had been seized by the desire to let himself be taken in tow, to jump on behind and ride along with the young man — to go himself riding a bit through the country, riding with flashing pedals into God's green world — hurray! — The wheel was not able to withstand this desperate drag for any length of time; it stood still, it wobbled, it fell over.

And then Life grew wild. It had lighted upon one foot; then it drew back its right arm and gave Herr Piepsam such a blow on the chest that he staggered back several paces. Then, with a voice which swelled into a threatening tone, it said: " You must be drunk, you fool! You must be off your head! If you dare to hold me up again, I'll give you a smash in the jaw —

146

do you hear? I'll break your neck! And don't you forget it! "

With this it turned its back upon Herr Piepsam,
gave an indignant tug to its cap, drawing it tighter
upon its head, and once more mounted its wheel. No,
it was certainly not at a loss for words. And the business of mounting succeeded as well as before. Again
it merely thrust down one foot, sat securely in the
saddle, and had the machine once more under full
control. Piepsam saw its back diminish more and
more rapidly.

He stood there panting and stared after Life. It did
not take a header, no accident overtook it, no tire
burst, and no stone lay in its path; lightly it sailed on.
And then Piepsam began to shout and to scold — one
might have called it a bellowing, for it was no longer a
human voice.

" You shall not ride there! " he cried. " You shall
not! You shall ride out there and not on the path to
the cemetery, do you hear? You get off — get off at
once! Oh, oh! I'll report you! I'll sue you! God! if
you would only take a tumble, if you would only fall
off, you windy brute, I would kick you, kick you in
the face with my boots, you damned rogue! . . ."

Never had the like been seen before! A man calling

bad names on the way to the cemetery, a man with a swollen face, bellowing, a man whose scolding renders him hopping mad, who cuts capers, throwing his arms and legs about, and seems unable to control himself. The wheel was really no longer in sight, yet Piepsam still raved and danced in the same spot.

" Hold him! hold him! He is riding on the path to the cemetery! You villain! You impudent clown! You damned ass! If I could only get hold of you, wouldn't I skin you alive, you silly ass, you stupid windbag, you tomfool, you ignorant bounder! — You get off! You get off this very instant! Will nobody kick him into the dirt, the scoundrel? — Riding for pleasure, eh? On the way to the cemetery! Knock him off his wheel, the damned oaf! Oh! Oh! If I only had you, what wouldn't I do? And what else? Eyes blue as lightning, eh? May the devil scratch them out of your face, you ignorant, ignorant, ignorant bounder! . . ."

Piepsam now took to language which is not to be repeated; he foamed, and poured forth in his cracked voice the most shameful terms of reprobation, while the contortions of his body continually increased. A couple of children with a basket and a terrier came over from the high-road; they climbed across the ditch, stood about the screaming man, and looked curiously into his distorted visage. A few labourers,

148

who worked on the new buildings in the vicinity, or had just begun their midday rest, also became attentive, and a number of men as well as some of the women who were mixing mortar came walking towards the group. But Piepsam continued to rave on; he was growing worse and worse. In his blind and insane rage he shook his fists towards heaven and in all directions, shook his legs convulsively, turned himself round and round, bent the knee and leaped into the air again, succumbing to his excessive efforts to shout as loud as possible. He did not pause a single moment in his tirade, he hardly took time to breathe, and it was really astonishing where all his language came from. His face was terribly swollen, his high hat sat far back on his neck, and his false shirt-front, which was not fastened, hung out of his waistcoat. He had long ago arrived at generalities and poured out things which had not the remotest connexion with the subject in hand. They dealt with his dissipated life and with religious matters, uttered in a most unsuitable tone and viciously intermingled with curse-words.

" Come on, come on, all of you! " he bellowed. " Not you, not only you, but the rest of you, you with the bicycle caps and eyes blue as lightning! I'll shout truths into your ear so that your blood will run cold

149

for ever, you windy rogues! . . . You grin, do you? Shrug your shoulders? . . . I drink . . . certainly I drink! I even guzzle, if you care to hear it! What does that mean? It's a long road that knows no turning! The day will come, you good-for-nothing rubbish, when God shall weigh all of us. . . . Oh! oh! The Son of Man will come in the clouds, you innocent *canaille,* and His justice is not of this world! He will cast you into the outermost darkness, you merry wretches, where there is howling and . . ."

He was now surrounded by quite an imposing group of people. A few laughed and a few looked at him with wrinkled brows. More workmen and several more mortar-women had come over from the buildings. A driver had got off his wagon, halting it upon the high-road, and, whip in hand, had also climbed across the ditch. A man took Piepsam by the arm and shook him, but that had no effect. A squad of soldiers marched by and, laughing, craned their necks to look at him. The terrier could no longer hold back, but braced his forelegs against the ground and, with his tail thrust between his legs, howled directly into his face.

Suddenly Lobgott Piepsam cried once more at the top of his voice: " You get off, you get off at once, you ignorant bounder! " described a half-circle with one
150

arm, and then collapsed. He lay there, suddenly struck dumb, a black heap amidst the curious. His cylindrical silk hat flew off, rebounded once from the ground, and also lay there.

Two masons bent over the immovable Piepsam and discussed the case in that whole-hearted and sensible tone common to working-men. Then one of them went off at a quick stride. Those who remained behind undertook a few more experiments with the unconscious one. One man dashed water in his face out of a bucket, another poured some brandy out of a bottle into the palm of his hand and rubbed Piepsam's temples with it. But these efforts were crowned with no success.

A short interval thus elapsed. Then wheels were heard, and a wagon came along the high-road. It was an ambulance, drawn by two pretty little horses and with a gigantic red cross painted on each side. It came to a halt, and two men in neat uniforms climbed down from the driver's seat, and while one went to the back part of the wagon to open it and to draw out the stretcher, the other rushed upon the path to the cemetery, pushed the staring crowd aside, and, with the help of one of the men, carried Herr Piepsam to the wagon. He was laid upon the stretcher and shoved into the wagon like a loaf of bread into an oven, whereupon the door snapped shut and the two uni-formed men climbed to the driver's seat again. All this was done with great precision, with a few practised turns of the hand, quick and adroit, as by trained apes.

And then Lobgott Piepsam was driven away.

1901

AT THE PROPHET'S

AT THE PROPHET'S

THERE are strange places, strange minds, strange regions of the spirit, lofty and poverty-stricken. Along the peripheries of the big cities, where the street-lights grow scarcer and the policemen walk in couples, you must climb the stairs in the houses until you cannot go any higher, climb into the attics under slanting roofs, where pale young geniuses, criminals of dreams, sit brooding with folded arms; climb into cheap and imposingly decorated studios, where lonely, rebel artists, consumed from within, hungry yet proud, contend with their latest and wildest ideals in clouds of cigarette smoke. Here is the end of things, here is ice, purity, and nothingness. Here no contract is valid, no concession, no consideration, no measure, and no value. Here the air has grown so thin, so chaste, that the miasmata of life can no longer thrive. Here stubbornness reigns, the uttermost logical con-clusion, the ego upon its desperate throne, freedom, madness, and death.

It was Good Friday, eight o'clock in the evening.

Several of the people whom Daniel had invited came at the same time. They had received invitations on quarto sheets, upon which there was an eagle which bore a naked rapier in its claws through the air, and which contained in a singular handwriting a request to participate in a kind of convention on Good Friday evening, when Daniel's proclamations were to be read. And so now they met at the appointed hour in the desolate and half-dark suburban street in front of the banal block of flats which contained the physical home of the prophet.

A few were acquainted with one another and exchanged greetings. These were a Polish artist and the thin girl who lived with him; a lyric poet, a tall, black-bearded Semite, with his heavy-limbed, pallid wife, who wore clothes like draperies; an individual who looked at once sickly and martial, being a spiritualist who was also a retired cavalry captain; and a young philosopher with the appearance of a kangaroo. Only the short-story writer, a gentleman with a stiff hat and a cultivated moustache, knew no one. He came from another sphere and had come here only accidentally. He had a certain relationship to life and a book of his was much read in middle-class circles. He was determined to behave in a strictly modest fashion, to be appreciative, and on the whole to act like one who is

156

merely tolerated. He followed the others into the house at a short distance.

They mounted the stairs, one after the other, supporting themselves on the cast-iron railing. They were silent, for they were people who knew the value of words and were not accustomed to talk needlessly. In the dim light of the little oil-lamps which stood upon the window-sills at every turn of the stairs, they read the names upon the door-plates of the flats as they went past. They mounted past the care-haunted abodes of an insurance official, a midwife, a laundress, an "agent," a chiropodist — quietly, without contempt, but estranged. They climbed up this narrow staircase hall as up some half-lighted shaft, full of confidence and without pausing, for from above, far up where one could go no higher, a faint glow greeted them, a soft and fugitive and errant glow from the highest altitudes.

Finally they stood at the goal, under the roof, in the light of six candles, which were burning in different candlesticks upon a little table covered by a faded little altar-cloth at the head of the stairs. On the door, which looked like the entrance to a store-room, there was a grey oblong of cardboard, on which was to be read the name " Daniel " in Roman letters, done with black chalk. They rang.

157

A boy with a large head and a friendly expression opened the door. He wore a new suit of blue cloth and polished top-boots, and carried a candle in his hand. He lighted them obliquely across the small, dark corridor into an unpapered garret-like room, which was quite empty save for a wooden clothes-rack. Without a word, but with a gesture which was accompanied by a stammering guttural sound, the boy indicated that the guests should take off their wraps, and when the short-story writer, out of a sense of general friendliness, asked him a question, it became evident that the child was dumb. Holding his light, he led the guests once more across the corridor to another door and let them enter. The short-story writer brought up the rear. He wore a cut-away and gloves and was determined to act as though in church.

The room they entered was moderately large and was filled by an awesome shimmering, swaying brightness, engendered by twenty or twenty-five lighted candles. A young girl, with a white turned-over collar and cuffs relieving her simple dress, stood close beside the door and gave her hand to all who entered. This was Maria Josefa, Daniel's sister, with her innocent but foolish face. The short-story writer knew her. He had met her at a literary tea. She had sat there upright, with her cup in her hand, and had spoken of her

158

brother with a clear voice full of devotion. She worshipped Daniel.

The short-story writer's eyes wandered about the room in search of him.

" He is not here," said Maria Josefa. " He is absent, I don't know where. But he will be here among us in spirit and follow the proclamations, word for word, when they are read."

" Who is going to read them? " asked the short-story writer, in a low, reverent voice. He was really in earnest about it. He was a well-meaning and modest person, venerating all the phenomena of life, and quite willing to learn and to revere what was worthy of being revered.

" A disciple of my brother's," answered Maria Josefa, " whom we are expecting from Switzerland. He is not here yet. He will be on hand at the right moment."

Opposite the door a large chalk drawing was visible in the candlelight. It stood upon the table, its upper edge leaning against the slanting ceiling. The drawing, which was done in a bold, violent manner, represented Napoleon, standing in a clumsy and despotic attitude in front of a fireplace warming his jack-booted feet. At the right of the entrance rose an altar-like shrine, upon which, between candles burning in silver candelabra, stood a painted holy figure, with outspread hands, and eyes turned upward. A *prie-dieu* stood in front of this, and on approaching it one observed, leaning upright against one of the feet of the holy figure, a small amateur photograph. This showed a young man of about thirty years with a tremendously high, pale, retreating forehead and a smooth-shaven, bony face, like that of a bird of prey, full of concentrated spirituality.

The writer of short stories paused for a while before this picture of Daniel; then he ventured cautiously farther into the room. Behind a large, round table, into whose polished yellow surface, surrounded by a wreath of laurel, the same sword-bearing eagle which had been seen on the invitations was burned, towered a severe, narrow chair of a spiry Gothic design like a throne and supreme seat among a number of low wooden stools. A long bench of rude carpentry, covered with some cheap stuff, extended along the roomy niche formed by wall and roof, and in this niche there was a low window. Presumably because the squat tiled stove had proved to be over-heated, the window was open, and presented a view of a segment of blue night, in the depths and distance of which the irregularly spaced gas-lamps lost themselves as yellow, glowing dots in ever greater intervals.

160

Opposite the window the room narrowed down to a kind of alcove-like chamber, which was lighted more brightly than the other part of this attic, and appeared to be used partly as study, partly as chapel. At the back of this room there was a couch, covered by a thinnish, washed-out stuff. To the right, one could see a curtained book-rack, on top of which burned candles in candelabra and oil-lamps of antique shape. To the left was set a white-covered table, upon which stood a crucifix, a seven-branched candlestick, a goblet filled with red wine, and a piece of plum-cake upon a plate.

In the foreground of this alcove there stood upon a low platform a column of gilded plaster, surmounted by an iron candelabrum; the capital of the column was covered by an altar-cloth of blood-red silk. And upon this rested a pile of manuscript sheets of folio size: Daniel's proclamations. A light-coloured wallpaper bedecked with little Empire wreaths covered the walls and the slanting part of the ceiling. Deathmasks, rose wreaths, a large, rusty sword, hung upon the walls, and besides the large picture of Napoleon, there were portraits, of various sorts, of Luther, Nietzsche, Moltke, Alexander the Sixth, Robespierre, and Savonarola distributed about the room.

"All this has been lived!" said Maria Josefa,

161

peering into the respectfully restrained visage of the short-story writer to see what effect these furnishings had produced. But in the mean time other guests had come, quietly and solemnly, and people began to seat themselves on benches and chairs, in hushed expectancy. In addition to those who had arrived first, there now sat there a fantastic draughtsman, with senile, infantile face, a limping lady, who was accustomed to introduce herself as one devoted to " erotics," and an unmarried young mother of noble birth, who had been cast out by her family. She was without any intellectual interests whatever, and had found hospitality in these circles solely upon the ground of her motherhood. There were also an elderly authoress and a deformed musician — all in all some twelve persons. The short-story writer had withdrawn into the window niche, and Maria Josefa sat on a chair close to the door, her hands lying upon her knees, side by side. And thus they waited for the disciple from Switzerland, who would be on hand at the right moment.

Suddenly another guest arrived — the rich lady who loved to visit such affairs as a kind of hobby. She had come from the fashionable part of the city in her silken coupé, out of her splendid mansion with the Gobelins and the door-casings of *giallo antico*, had climbed up all the stairs, and now came through the

162

door, beautiful, fragrant, luxurious, in a dress of blue cloth with yellow embroidery, a Parisian hat upon her reddish brown hair, and a smile in her Titian eyes. She came out of curiosity, out of ennui, out of joy in contrarieties, out of sheer goodwill towards all that was a little out of the common, out of a kindly extravagance of feelings. She greeted Daniel's sister and the short-story writer, who was frequently a guest at her house, and then seated herself on the bench in front of the window niche between the erotic lady and the philosopher who had the appearance of a kangaroo, as though that was all quite in order.

" I've almost come too late," said she softly with her beautiful, mobile mouth to the short-story writer, who sat behind her. " I had people to tea, and so things dragged along."

The short-story writer was much affected and thanked Heaven that he was in a presentable dress. " How beautiful she is! " thought he. " She is worthy of being the mother of that daughter of hers."

" And Fräulein Sonia? " he asked her across her shoulder. " Didn't you bring Fräulein Sonia with you? "

Sonia was the daughter of the rich lady, and in the eyes of the short-story writer she was an unbelievable example of a perfect creature, a marvel of versatile

163

education, an attained ideal of culture. He spoke her name twice, for it gave him an inexpressible pleasure to pronounce it.

" Sonia is ill," said the rich lady. " Yes — would you believe it? — she has a bad foot. Oh, it is nothing, a swelling, a kind of little inflammation or congestion. It has been cut. It might not have been necessary, perhaps, but she insisted upon it herself."

" She insisted upon it herself! " repeated the short-story writer in an enthusiastic whisper. " That is like her! But how in the world can one express one's sympathy? "

" Well, I'll take her your greetings! " said the rich woman. And as he was silent, she added: " Doesn't that satisfy you? "

" No, it does not," said he very softly, and as she prized his books, she answered with a smile:

" Well, then, send her a flower or two."

" Thanks! " said he. " Thanks! I'll do so! " And he thought to himself: " A flower or two? A nosegay! A big bouquet! I'll drive tomorrow to the florist's before breakfast! " And he felt that he had a certain relation to life.

A slight noise was heard without, the door opened and closed quickly and with a jerk, and a short and stocky young man in a dark lounge-suit stood before

the guests in the candlelight: the disciple from Switzerland. He cast a swift and threatening look over the
room, strode with heavy steps towards the plaster column in front of the alcove, established himself behind
this on the low platform with a firmness as though he
wished to take root there, seized the uppermost sheet
of manuscript, and instantly began to read.

He was about twenty-eight years of age, short-
necked, and ugly. His cropped hair grew in the form
of an acute point unusually far down on his forehead,
which besides was low and furrowed. His face, beard-
less, sullen, and heavy, revealed a doglike nose,
coarse cheek-bones, a pair of sunken cheeks, and
coarse, protuberant lips, which seemed to shape the
words they spoke only by a great effort, reluctantly,
and with a kind of limp anger. His face was brutal
and yet pale. He read with a wild and overloud voice,
which, however, at the same time trembled inwardly,
shook, and suffered from scantiness of breath. The
hand that held the written sheet was broad and red,
and yet it trembled. He embodied an eerie mixture of
brutality and weakness, and the things he read coincided in a strange way with his looks.

They were sermons, comparisons, theses, laws, vi-
sions, prophecies, and appeals in the manner of orders of the day, and these followed one another in a

variegated and endless string, in a mixture of styles, in tones borrowed from the Psalms and from Revelation, intermingled with military-strategic as well as philosophical-critical "trade" expressions. A feverish ego, terribly excited, thrust itself upward in solitary megalomania and threatened the world with a torrent of convulsive words. *Christus imperator maximus* was his name and he recruited death-devoted troops for the subjugation of the terrestrial globe, issued messages, set up his implacable conditions, longed for poverty and chastity, and in a spirit of boundless revolt kept on reiterating with a kind of unnatural lust the imperative of unconditional obedience. Buddha, Alexander, Napoleon, and Jesus were all designated as his humble predecessors, not worthy of unloosing the shoe-latchets of this spiritual emperor.

The disciple read for an hour; then, trembling, he took a gulp from the goblet of red wine and reached for new proclamations. Sweat stood in pearls on his low forehead, his thick lips quivered, and between the words he kept on blowing his breath with a short, snorting sound through his nose, like a bellowing exhaust. The solitary ego sang, raved, and commanded. It lost itself in mad metaphors, went down in a whirl of illogic, and suddenly popped up again horribly and quite unexpectedly in another place. Blasphemies and

166

hosannas, incense and fumes of blood, were intermingled. The world was conquered in thunderous battles and then redeemed.

It would have been difficult to establish the effect of Daniel's proclamations upon the auditors. Some of them, with heads thrown back, looked with lack-lustre eyes at the ceiling; others, bent over their knees, held their faces buried in their hands. The eyes of the lady devoted to " erotics " grew dim in a peculiar manner every time the word " chastity " was spoken, and the philosopher with the appearance of a kangaroo now and again described something vague in the air with his long and crooked index finger. The short-story writer had for a long time been seeking in vain some adequate support for his aching back. At ten o'clock he was visited by the vision of a ham sandwich, but he shied this off manfully.

About half past ten one saw that the disciple held the last folio sheet in his red and trembling right hand. He had finished. " Soldiers! " he wound up, with the last ounce of his strength, with a failing voice of thunder, " I deliver unto you to be plundered — the world! " He then stepped down from the platform, regarded everybody with a threatening look, and vanished as violently as he had come, through the door.

The audience remained for a moment immovably

167

in the position which they had last assumed. Then, as with a common resolve, they stood up and went away immediately, after each, with a soft word or two, had pressed the hand of Maria Josefa, who, innocent and calm, again stood in her white collar close beside the door.

The dumb lad was on hand outside. He lighted the guests to the cloak-room, helped them to put on their wraps, and led them through the narrow hall with the staircase, upon which, from the supreme height of Daniel's realm, the moving light of the candles fell, down to the house door, which he unlocked. The guests, one after the other, stepped out upon the desolate suburban street.

The coupé of the rich lady had halted in front of the house. One saw how the coachman on the box between the two brilliant lanterns touched his hat with his whip-hand. The short-story writer accompanied the rich lady to the carriage door.

" How did you stand it? " he asked.

" I don't like to express an opinion upon such things," she replied. " Perhaps he is really a genius, or something similar."

" Yes, what is genius? " he asked thoughtfully. " All requirements are present in this Daniel — loneliness, freedom, intellectual passion, magnificent visual capacity, belief in himself, even the proximity of crime and madness. What is lacking? Possibly the human? A little feeling, longing, love? But that is an entirely improvised hypothesis.

"Give Sonia my greetings," he said as she reached him her hand in farewell after seating herself, and he studied her face intently to see how she would take his speaking simply of "Sonia," not of "Fräulein Sonia," or of "your daughter."

She prized his books, and so she suffered it with a smile.

"I'll do so."

"Thanks!" said he, and a whirl of hope bewildered him. "And now I'll eat supper like a wolf!"

He had a certain relationship to life.

1904

LITTLE LOUISE

LITTLE LOUISE

THERE are marriages the origin of which not even the most practised literary imagination could possibly conceive. One must accept them as one accepts adventurous combinations of contrary qualities in the theatre — such as old and stupid with beautiful and vivacious — which are given as assumptions and serve as the basis for the mathematical composition of a farce.

As to the wife of Herr Jacoby, counsellor-at-law, she was young and beautiful, a woman of unusual charms. Some, let us say, thirty years ago she had been christened with the names Anna, Marguerite, Rose, Amalie, but she had always been called Amra, a name composed of the initial letters of all these names, a name which with its exotic ring fitted her personality like no other. For though the darkness of her thick, soft hair, which was parted on the side and drawn back along both sides of her narrow forehead, was only the darkness of the chestnut kernel, her skin revealed a perfect southern smooth and shadowy olive, and this skin covered contours which also seemed to have ripened in a southern sun, and which reminded one of the vegetative and lazy voluptuousness of a sultana. This impression, which was provoked by all of her indolent, sensual movements, also coincided with the likelihood that her reason was subordinated to her heart. One look from her ingenuous, brown eyes, as she drew up her pretty eyebrows towards her almost pathetically low forehead in her original way, was enough to convince one of that. But she, too, knew this — she was not too simple for that — she simply avoided exposing herself, by speaking little and seldom; and there is nothing to be said against a woman who is pretty and silent. Oh, that word " simple " was surely least expressive of her. Her look was not only foolish, but also of a certain avid slyness, and one could see plainly that this woman was not too limited in intellect to be inclined to make trouble. — As for the rest, her nose seen in profile may have been a bit too large and fleshy; but her broad, full mouth was quite perfect, even though without any expression save that of sensuality.

This perilous woman was the wife of Counsellor-at-law Jacoby, who was about forty years of age — and whoever saw him was astounded. He was stout, was the counsellor-at-law, he was more than stout; he was a veritable colossus of a man! His legs, which were always clad in ash-grey trousers, reminded one by their columnar formlessness of those of an elephant; his back, rounded by bolsters of fat, was like that of a bear; and the queer grey-green knitted jacket which he was accustomed to wear was fastened so painfully across the monstrous curve of his stomach, by a single button, that it sprang back on both sides as far as his shoulders as soon as the button was undone. Upon this tremendous torso, almost without the intermediation of a neck, there was perched a relatively small head with tiny and watery eyes, a short, stubby nose, and jowls pendulous with flesh, between which a minute mouth with sadly drooping corners was almost lost. The round skull as well as the upper lip was covered with sparse and wiry, light-blond bristles, which permitted the naked skin to shine through everywhere, as with an overfed dog. — Ah, yes, it must have been clear to all the world that the corpulence of the counsellor-at-law was not of a healthy nature. His huge body, as long as it was broad, was over-fat, without being muscular, and one could frequently observe how a sudden access of blood would rush into his congested face and give way just as suddenly to a yellow pallor, while his mouth was distorted in a sourish way.

The practice of the counsellor-at-law was very limited; but as he had a considerable fortune, in part from his wife, the couple — who were, moreover, childless — occupied a very comfortable flat in the Kaiserstrasse and kept up a good deal of social intercourse; chiefly, to be sure, to gratify Frau Amra's wishes, for it is impossible that the counsellor-at-law, who seemed to participate only with a kind of tortured enthusiasm, took any pleasure in these affairs. The character of this fat man was most peculiar. No man living could have been more polite, more obliging, more yielding towards everybody, than he; but though one did not speak of it, perhaps, one felt that his over-friendly and flattering attitude was for one reason or another forced, that it was based upon timidity and lack of inner poise, and this affected one disagreeably. No spectacle is more unlovely than that of a man who despises himself, but who nevertheless out of cowardice and vanity would like to be amiable and to please; and, in my opinion, it was not otherwise with the counsellor-at-law, who went too far in his almost grovelling self-deprecation, so that he was utterly unable to keep the necessary amount of personal dignity. He was capable of saying to a lady whom he wished to escort to the table: " Dear madam, I am a disgusting person, but won't you do me the honour? "

176

And, having no gift for self-mockery, he would say this in a bitter-sweet, tortured, repulsive manner.

The following anecdote is also based on fact: One day as the counsellor-at-law was out walking, a rough porter with a hand-cart came along and drove one wheel violently over his foot. The man stopped the cart too late and turned round — whereupon the counsellor-at-law, losing all control of himself, pale and with trembling cheeks, took off his hat with a profound bow and stammered: " I beg your pardon! " — Things of that sort evoke indignation. Yet this singular colossus seemed to be eternally plagued by an evil conscience. When he appeared with his wife on the Lerchenberg, the main promenade of the town, he greeted all and sundry — while now and then he cast a shy glance at Amra, striding with such wonderful elasticity at his side — as over-earnestly, timidly, and zealously as though he felt the need of bowing humbly to every lieutenant and begging forgiveness that he, precisely he, should be in possession of this beautiful woman; and the pathetically friendly expression of his mouth seemed to beg one not to make fun of him.

It has already been indicated that it is a question why precisely Amra should have married Counsellor-at-law Jacoby. He, on his part, loved her, and that

177

with a love so passionate as is surely seldom found in people of his physique, and yet this love was humble and timid in accordance with the rest of his nature. Often, late at night, when Amra had already gone to rest in the big bedroom, the high windows of which were draped by flowered curtains that fell in plentiful folds, the counsellor-at-law would steal to the side of her heavy bed, so softly that one could not hear his footsteps, but merely felt the slow trembling of the floor and the furniture, kneel down, and with infinite care seize her hand. At such times Amra would draw up her eyebrows and regard her husband, who lay before her in the weak light of the night-lamp, silently and with an expression of sensual malice. But he, while he carefully drew back the chemise from her shoulder with his plump and trembling hands and buried his fat, sorrowful face in the soft hollow of her full and olive-coloured arm, there where small, blue veins stood relieved against the dark skin — he would begin to speak in a suppressed and trembling voice, to speak as a sensible person is really never accustomed to speak in everyday life.

"Amra," he would whisper, "my dear Amra! I am not disturbing you? You were not sleeping yet? Great God, I have thought the whole day long how beautiful you are and how I love you! — Listen to

178

what I want to tell you; it is so difficult to express it
— I love you so much that my heart sometimes con-
tracts with pain and I don't know where to go; I love
you beyond my powers! No doubt you don't understand this, but you must believe me, and you must tell
me just once that you will be a bit thankful to me for
that; for, you see, such a love as mine for you is something worth while in this life — and that you will
never betray or deceive me, even though you can't
love me, but out of gratitude, out of sheer gratitude
— I come to you to beg this of you with all my heart
and soul."

And such confessions would usually end by the
counsellor-at-law's beginning to weep softly and bitterly, without altering his position. In this instance,
however, Amra was moved, passed her hand a-
cross the bristles of her husband's hand, and said
several times in that long-drawn, comforting, and
mocking tone in which one speaks to a dog that
comes to lick one's feet: " There! There! Good old
fellow! "

This behaviour of Amra's was certainly not that of
a moral woman. And it is now high time that I should
release the truth that I have kept back up to the present; the fact, namely, that she was, after all, false
to her husband; that she deceived him, I say, with a

gentleman named Alfred Läutner. This was a young and gifted musician, who had already at twenty-seven years of age achieved a pretty reputation by means of amusing little compositions; a slender fellow with an impertinent face, a mop of blond hair, and in his eyes a sunny smile, which was very self-conscious. He belonged to that class of small artists of today who do not demand too much of themselves, who wish in the first instance to be happy and charming persons, who make use of their agreeable little talents to augment their personal popularity, and who love to play the naïve genius in society. Consciously childish, immoral, unscrupulous, merry, self-satisfied as they are, and healthy enough to find themselves interesting even in their illnesses, their vanity becomes, in fact, charming so long as it has never been wounded. But woe to these petty mimes and happy ones when they are overtaken by a serious misfortune, a sorrow which does not permit itself to be coquetted with, in which they can no longer be amused! They will not understand how to be unhappy in a respectable manner, they will not know what to " set about " with their sorrow, they will go to ruin — but that is a story by itself. — Herr Läutner composed pretty things: waltzes and mazurkas mostly, the gaiety of which was a bit too popular (so far as I understand these things) for them to be accounted as real music, had it not been that each of these compositions contained some small original bit, a modulation, an interlude, a harmonious turn, some tiny effect that operated upon the nerves, that betrayed cleverness and invention. They appeared to be composed for this end, and this also made them interesting for serious connoisseurs. Often these two solitary measures had something wonderfully pathetic and melancholy about them, something that suddenly rang forth and quickly ebbed away in the dance-hall gaiety of these little compositions.

It was for this young man that Amra Jacoby burned with an illicit passion, and he on his part had not possessed enough moral strength to resist her lures. They met here, they met there, and an unchaste relationship had bound the two together for over a year, a relationship known to the whole town and about which the entire town gossiped behind the back of the counsellor-at-law. And as for himself? Amra was too stupid to suffer from an evil conscience and to betray herself through this. It must be accepted as a matter of fact that the counsellor-at-law, however much his heart may always have been oppressed by care and fear, could not cherish any definite suspicion of his wife.

SPRING had come to rejoice every heart, and Amra had had a most agreeable idea.

"Christian," said she — the counsellor-at-law was named Christian — "let us give a party, a big party, in honour of the newly-brewed spring beer — of course, a very simple affair, just cold roast veal, but with a lot of people."

"Certainly," answered the counsellor-at-law. "But couldn't we perhaps postpone it for a bit?"

Amra did not reply to this, but at once went into details. "There will be so many people, you know, that our rooms here will be too small. We must rent some establishment or garden or hall outside the city, so as to have sufficient room and fresh air. You will realize that. I am thinking, first of all, of that large hall of Herr Wendelin's, at the foot of the Lerchenberg. This hall stands free and is connected only by a passage with the actual restaurant and the brewery. It could be decorated in a festal way; long tables could be set up there and spring beer drunk. One could dance there and make music, perhaps also do some light theatricals, for I know there is a small stage there — I am particularly keen on that. — Well, in one word, it must be a most original party, and we shall have a wonderful good time."

The face of the counsellor-at-law had grown a pale

yellow during this recital, and the corners of his mouth were drawn downwards. He said: " I'm heartily glad to hear it, my dear Amra. I know that I can leave it all to your cleverness. Please make your arrangements."

AND Amra made her arrangements. She consulted with various ladies and gentlemen, she personally rented Herr Wendelin's large hall, she formed a kind of committee of people who had been asked or had volunteered to take part in the merry proceedings which were to embellish the party. This committee was composed wholly of gentlemen, with the exception of the wife of Herr Hildebrandt, an actor at the Theatre Royal; she was a singer. There were, in addition, Herr Hildebrandt himself, a certain barrister Witznagel, a young painter, and Herr Alfred Läutner, not to forget a number of students who had been introduced by the barrister and were to execute nigger dances.

A week after Amra had made up her mind, this committee had assembled for purposes of deliberation in the Kaiserstrasse — to be quite exact, in Amra's drawing-room, a small, warm, and well-fitted room, which was furnished with a thick carpet, a sofa with many cushions, a fan-palm, English arm-chairs of leather, and a mahogany table with curved legs, on which lay a plush table-cloth and several *de luxe* books. There was also a fireplace, in which a small fire still glowed; on the black marble mantelpiece stood several plates with dainty little sandwiches, glasses, and two carafes of sherry.

Amra, with one foot lightly poised upon the other, leaned back on the cushions of the sofa, which was over-shadowed by the fan-palm, and was as fair as a night in June. She wore a blouse of light and very thin silk, but her skirt was of a heavy, dark material, embroidered with large flowers. Now and then she brushed back a curl of chestnut hair from her narrow forehead. — Frau Hildebrandt, the singer, also sat upon the sofa beside her; she had red hair and was in riding-costume. Opposite the two ladies the gentlemen had seated themselves in a crowded half-circle — in the midst of them the counsellor-at-law, who had found only a very low leather arm-chair and seemed unutterably unhappy; now and then he drew a deep breath and swallowed, as though he were fighting against an encroaching nausea. — Herr Alfred Läutner, in tennis rig, had resigned all claims to a chair and stood leaning elegantly and good-humouredly against the mantelpiece, for he had declared that he could not sit quietly so long.

184

Herr Hildebrandt spoke with an agreeable voice about English songs. He was an extremely respectable and worthy man, dressed in black, with a massive Cæsarean head and a certain aplomb in his carriage — a court actor of culture, solid knowledge, and refined taste. He was fond of condemning Ibsen, Zola, and Tolstoy in earnest conversations, for he held that all of them were bent upon the same sinister purpose; today, however, he was engaged condescendingly in the trifling matter under discussion.

" May I ask whether the ladies and gentlemen know that delightful song, ' That's Maria '? " he asked. " It is a bit piquant, but of most uncommon effectiveness. And then there is that famous — " and he proposed a few additional songs, upon which they finally agreed, and which Frau Hildebrandt consented to sing. — The young painter, a gentleman with extremely sloping shoulders and a blond Vandyke beard, was to parody a magician, while Herr Hildebrandt intended to portray famous men — in short, everything evolved in the most favourable manner, and the program seemed to be already complete, when Barrister Witznagel, who owned most courteous movements and many duelling-scars, suddenly opened the discussion again.

" All very fine, ladies and gentlemen, everything promises to be really entertaining. However, I feel I

185

must touch upon one point. It seems to me that something is still lacking, and indeed the chief feature, the star turn, the *clou,* the climax — something most special, something startling, a comic turn which will cap the fun — in short, I make the suggestion, I have no definite idea; but according to my feelings — "

" That is really so! " Herr Läutner let his tenor voice be heard from the direction of the fireplace. " Witznagel is right. A main turn, a closing feature, would be most desirable. Let's consider! " And while he adjusted his red belt with a swift twist or two, he looked inquiringly about him. The expression of his face was really most affable.

" Of course," said Herr Hildebrandt, " if one does not care to let the famous men be the climax — "

All agreed with the young barrister. It would be most desirable to have a specially comic leading turn. Even the counsellor-at-law nodded and said softly: " Quite right — something predominantly gay — " All began to ponder over the problem.

And it was at the close of this pause in the conversation, which lasted about a minute and which was interrupted only by short exclamations attendant upon deliberation, that the remarkable thing occurred. Amra sat leaning back among the cushions of the sofa, and was gnawing nimbly and eagerly as a mouse at the pointed nail of her little finger, while her face betrayed a most extraordinary expression. A smile played about her lips, an absent and almost delirious smile, which revealed a painful as well as cruel lust, and her eyes, which were wide open and shining, wandered slowly towards the mantelpiece, where they remained for a moment fixed upon those of the young musician. Then with a sudden flounce she flung the upper part of her body to one side, towards her husband, the counsellor-at-law, and, both hands in her lap, stared him in the face with a look that seemed to clutch and draw him, while her face grew visibly paler. She spoke in a full, slow voice: " Christian, I propose that at the close you appear as a *chanteuse* in a baby-dress of red silk and dance something for us."

The effect of these few words was enormous. Only the young painter strove to laugh good-humouredly. Herr Hildebrandt, with a face as cold as stone, picked invisible fluff from his sleeve; the students coughed and used their handkerchiefs with unseemly loudness. Frau Hildebrandt blushed violently, which did not often occur, and Herr Witznagel, the barrister, simply ran off, to get a sandwich. The counsellor-at-law squatted in a torturous position upon his low armchair and looked about him with a yellow face and an anxious smile, while he stammered: " But, my God —

I — am really not capable — not as though — you must forgive me — "

Alfred Läutner's face was without a care no longer. It looked as though he was a little flushed, and with his head thrust forward he peered into Amra's eyes, disturbed, uncomprehending, searching.

But she, Amra, without altering her aggressive position, continued to speak, with the same weighty emphasis: " And you must sing a song, Christian, which Herr Läutner has composed, and which he will accompany on the piano; that will prove the best and most effective climax of our party."

A pause ensued, an oppressive pause. But then, quite suddenly and strangely, Herr Läutner, similarly infected, carried away and excited, made a step forward, and, trembling with a kind of swift enthusiasm, began to speak rapidly: " By God, Herr Jacoby, I am ready, I am really ready to compose something for you. You must sing it, you must dance it. It is the only thinkable climax of the party. You'll see, you'll see — it will be the best thing I've done or ever can do. In a baby-dress of red silk! Ah, your wife is an artist, an artist, I tell you, or she could never have hit upon this idea! Do say yes, I beg you, say you'll agree! I'll accomplish something, I'll do something, you'll see! "

188

This relieved the tension and everybody joined in. Either out of malice or out of politeness, all began to besiege the counsellor-at-law, and Frau Hildebrandt went so far as to say aloud, in her best Brünhilde voice: "Herr Jacoby, you are usually such a merry and entertaining man!" But the counsellor-at-law himself now found his tongue, and, still a trifle yellow, but with a great show of decisiveness, he declared: "Listen to me, ladies and gentlemen! — what shall I say to you? I'm not suited for it, believe me! I have almost no comic aptitude, and quite apart from that — in short, no, it is really impossible."

He stubbornly persisted in this refusal, and as Amra took no more part in the conversation, and sat leaning back with a rather absent expression on her face, and as Herr Läutner did not speak another word, but fixedly contemplated an arabesque in the carpet, Herr Hildebrandt succeeded in giving another turn to the talk, and soon afterwards the company broke up, without having reached any decision on the last question.

On the evening of the same day, however, after Amra had gone to bed and lay there with open eyes, her husband came in with heavy tread, drew up a chair beside her bed, sat down, and said softly and hesitatingly: "Listen, Amra, to be quite open, I am worried

189

by doubts. If I happened to be in any way disobliging to those ladies and gentlemen today, if I offended them — God knows it was not my intention! Or do you seriously believe — I beg you — "

Amra was silent for a moment, while her eyebrows slowly rose towards her forehead. She then shrugged her shoulders and said: " I don't know what I should say, my dear man. You behaved as I should never have expected of you. You refused in discourteous terms to support the entertainment by your co-operation, which everybody considered necessary. That can be only flattering to you. To put it mildly, you disappointed everybody very much, and you have upset the whole party by your being so rude and disobliging, whereas it was your duty as host — "

The counsellor-at-law hung his head, and, breathing heavily, he said: " No, Amra. I really did not wish to be disobliging, believe me. I don't want to offend anyone or displease anyone, and if I have acted unkindly, I am ready to make amends. It is only a lark, a bit of mummery, a harmless joke — why not? I don't want to upset the party, I am ready — "

The following afternoon Amra drove out once again, to attend to some " shopping." She stopped the carriage at No. 78 in the Holzstrasse and went up to

190

the second story, where someone was waiting for her. And as she lay there, abandoned to love, and pressed his head to her breast, she whispered passionately: " Compose it for four hands, do you hear? We will accompany him together while he sings and dances. I, I will attend to the costume — "

And a strange thrill, a suppressed and convulsive laughter, shot through the bodies of both.

To all those who wish to give a party, an alfresco entertainment on a large scale, it is strongly recommended to look up the establishment of Herr Wendelin on the Lerchenberg. You leave the pretty suburban street and pass through a high gateway into a park-like garden, belonging to the establishment. The spacious festal hall stands in the centre of this park. This hall, which is connected by a narrow passage with the restaurant, the kitchen, and the brewery, is built of wood, gaily painted in a droll mixture of Chinese and Renaissance styles. There are two wide swing-doors, which can be left open in fair weather, so as to admit the breath of the trees. The hall is capable of holding a great many people.

Tonight the carriages, as they came rolling on, were greeted even from afar by a glow of coloured light, for the entire enclosure, the trees of the garden, and the hall itself were decorated with coloured lanterns in close rows. And as to the inside of the hall itself, this offered a really delightful spectacle. Thick garlands were festooned across the ceiling, and to these in turn still more paper lanterns were fastened, though a great number of electric bulbs gleamed forth between the decorations of the walls, which consisted of flags, greenery, and artificial flowers, and these lighted up the hall most brilliantly. The stage was situated at one end, with potted plants standing on both sides of it, and a genius, painted by some artist, floated on the expanse of the red curtain. The long tables, decorated with flowers, extended from the other end of the hall almost to the stage, and here the guests of Herr Jacoby, counsellor-at-law, regaled themselves with spring beer and roast veal — lawyers, officers, merchants, artists, upper officials, as well as their wives and daughters — surely more than a hundred and fifty persons. They were dressed quite informally, in dark suits and spring dresses not too light in colour, for merry unconstraint was the rule of the evening. The gentlemen went personally with mugs to the big barrels, which stood along one of the side walls; and the bright, spacious, and gaily coloured hall, which was permeated by the sweetish and sultry festal odour of pine-branches, flowers, hu-

man beings, beer, and food, hummed and buzzed with
the clatter, the loud and simple talk, the clear, lively,
polite, and care-free laughter of all these people. The
counsellor-at-law sat, an uncouth, helpless mass at the
end of a table, near the stage. He drank little, and now
and then he laboriously addressed a few words to his
neighbour, Frau Havermann, wife of a government
councillor. He breathed with difficulty, the corners of
his mouth were drawn down, and his protruding, turbid, watery eyes looked immovably and with a kind
of melancholy amazement on this merry to-do, as
though there was something unutterably sad and incomprehensible in this atmosphere of festivity, this
noisy merriment.

Large, rich cakes were now served, and the guests
began to drink sweet wines and to make speeches.
Herr Hildebrandt, the court actor, did honour to the
spring beer in a speech which consisted entirely of
classical quotations, yes, even from the Greek, and
Herr Witznagel, the barrister, using his most agreeable gestures and his most exquisite language, toasted
the ladies present. He seized a handful of flowers
from the nearest vase and from the table-cloth, and
compared each with a lady. Amra Jacoby, who sat
opposite him in an evening dress of thin, yellow silk,
was called " the lovelier sister of the tea-rose."

Immediately after this she passed her hand over the parting of her soft hair and earnestly nodded towards her husband — whereupon the ponderous man stood up and almost spoiled the spirits of everybody by the painful manner and hideous smile with which he stammered a few paltry words. Only a few artificial bravos were heard, and an oppressive silence reigned for a moment. At once, however, merriment again held sway, and the guests, smoking and rather enlivened by drink, began to rise and, with considerable noise, to move the tables from the hall themselves, for they wanted to dance.

It was past eleven o'clock, and the last trace of formality had vanished. A part of the company had poured forth into the gaily lighted garden to enjoy the fresh air, while the others remained in the hall, standing about in groups, smoking, chatting, filling their beer-glasses, and drinking as they stood. Then a loud trumpet-blast sounded from the stage, calling everybody into the hall. Musicians — a string and brass band — had arrived and had disposed themselves in front of the curtain. Rows of chairs, each with a red program lying on it, had been placed, and the ladies seated themselves, while the gentlemen stood behind them or along both sides of the hall. An expectant silence reigned.

The small orchestra played a rushing overture, the curtain parted — and, behold, there stood a number of hideous Negroes, in screaming costumes and with blood-red lips, who gnashed their teeth and raised a barbaric howl. — These performances were, in fact, the climax of Amra's party. Enthusiastic applause burst forth, and the cleverly arranged program proceeded, number by number. Frau Hildebrandt appeared in a powdered wig, prodded the floor with a long cane, and sang in an over-loud voice: " That's Maria! " A magician appeared in a dress-suit covered with orders and did most astonishing things. Herr Hildebrandt represented Goethe, Bismarck, and Napoleon in a startlingly realistic maner, and Doctor Wiesensprung, editor of a paper, undertook at the last moment to deliver a humorous lecture on the theme: " Spring beer and its social significance." Towards the close, however, the tension attained its maximum, for now the final number was due, that mysterious number which was surrounded by a laurel wreath on the program and described as " Little Louise. Song and Dance. Music by Alfred Läutner."

A stir went through the hall, and eyes met eyes as the musicians put aside their instruments, and Herr Läutner, who up to this moment had been silently leaning against a door with a cigarette between his carelessly pursed-up lips, took his place with Amra Jacoby at the piano, which stood in the centre of the stage before the curtain. His face was flushed, and he turned the pages of written notes nervously, while Amra, who, on the contrary, was a little pale, looked at the audience with a lowering look, one arm supported on the back of the chair. Then, as all necks were being craned, the shrill tinkle of the bell was heard. Herr Läutner and Amra played a few bars of an indifferent introduction, the curtain rolled upward, Little Louise appeared —

As this sorry and horribly dressed-up mass came on with laborious steps, like those of a dancing bear, a shock of astonishment and cold horror went through the crowd of on-lookers. It was the counsellor-at-law. A wide dress of blood-red silk, without folds, which reached to his feet, invested his shapeless body, and this dress was *décolleté*, so that his throat, touched with powder, was exposed unpleasantly. The sleeves were very short and puffed at the shoulders, and long, light yellow gloves covered the thick and muscular arms. A high, flaxen wig with ringlets, in which a green feather nodded to and fro, was perched on his head. From beneath this wig a yellow, distorted, unhappy, and desperately merry face peered forth, the

196

cheeks continually bobbing up and down in a way that moved one to pity. The small, red-rimmed eyes stared fixedly at the floor, without seeing anything, while the fat man threw his weight ponderously, first on one foot, then on the other, either holding his dress with both hands or raising his two forefingers with feeble arms — he knew no other gesture — and in a strained and panting voice sang a silly song to the sound of the piano.

Did not, more than ever, a cold breath of suffering emanate from this pathetic figure, a breath which killed all easy-going joyousness and oppressed the entire company as with an inevitable burden of painful atmosphere? The same horror lay in the depths of all the countless eyes which were fixed as by a spell direct upon this picture, on this pair at the piano and on this husband up there. This quiet, incredible scandal lasted at least five long minutes.

But then came the moment which no one that experienced it will forget as long as he lives. — Let us make clear to ourselves what really happened in this short, terrible, and complicated space of time.

Everybody knows the ridiculous song that is entitled " Little Louise," and everybody remembers, no doubt, the lines which run:

" To polka and to waltz I rally,
  And dance them as none other can;
  Little Louise from down our alley,
  Who charms the heart of every man "

— unlovely and frivolous verses which form the refrain to three rather long stanzas. Well, in composing
these words anew, Alfred Läutner had accomplished
his masterpiece, by making the most of his habit of
startling one by introducing an artistic piece of lofty
music in the very midst of vulgar and comic claptrap.
The melody, which had been pitched in C-sharp major,
had been rather pretty and utterly banal during the
first stanzas. At the beginning of the refrain quoted,
the time grew livelier, and discords cropped up which
led one to expect a modulation to F-sharp major
through the increasingly vivacious sounding forth of
a B. These disharmonies grew complicated up to the
words " other can," and after the " Little," which
completed the complication and the suspension, there
should have followed a resolution in F-sharp major.
Instead of this something most surprising occurred.
By means of a sudden turn, due to a most ingenious
idea, the key suddenly altered to F major, and this in-
terpolation, which followed on the second syllable of
the word " Louise," long drawn out by means of both

pedals, was of an indescribable, absolutely unheard-of effect! It was a sudden attack, a perfectly amazing onslaught, upon the nerves, which sent thrills down the spine; it was a marvel, an exposure, an unveiling almost cruel in its suddenness, a curtain that was rent.

At this F-major chord the counsellor-at-law Jacoby stopped dancing. He stood still, stood in the centre of the stage as though rooted there, both forefingers still raised — one a little lower than the other — the " i " of " Louise " broke from his lips, and he grew silent. The piano accompaniment broke off sharply at the same time, while this daring and horribly ridiculous apparition up there stared straight in front of him, with head thrust forth in an animal-like way and with inflamed eyes. He stared into this decorated, bright, and crowded festal hall, in which, like an emanation of all these people, scandal lay packed like some dense atmosphere. He stared into all these raised, distorted, and sharply lighted faces, into these hundreds of eyes, which were all fixed on himself and on the couple below and before him with the same knowing expression. While a terrible silence, unbroken by a single sound, lay over all, he let his eyes, growing ever wider, wander slowly and eerily from the couple to the audience and from the audience to the couple. A sudden insight seemed to pass over his face, and it was suddenly suffused with a rush of blood, which caused it to grow congested and as red as the silk dress, and left it as yellow as wax immediately after — and the stout man collapsed, making the boards rattle.

The silence continued for a moment; then cries were heard, a tumult arose, a few bold men, among them a young physician, sprang from the orchestra to the stage, the curtain was dropped.

Amra Jacoby and Alfred Läutner still sat at the piano, turned away from each other. He, with lowered head, still seemed to be listening to his modulation to F major; she, incapable of apprehending so rapidly with her birdlike brain what had happened, stared about her with a perfectly vacant face.

The young doctor reappeared immediately in the hall — a small Jewish gentleman with serious face and black, pointed beard. To a number of gentlemen who crowded round him at the door he answered, with a shrug of his shoulders: " All over."

1897

LITTLE HERR FRIEDEMANN

LITTLE HERR FRIEDEMANN

It was the fault of the wet-nurse. What was the good of Frau Consul Friedemann's giving her an earnest talking-to, when her suspicions were first aroused, and bidding her suppress that vice of hers? What was the good of giving her a daily glass of claret in addition to the nourishing beer? It was suddenly evident that this young woman also went so far as to drink the spirits intended for the cooking-stove, and before a substitute for her had arrived, before one could discharge her, the disaster had happened. One day when the mother and her three half-grown daughters returned from a walk, little Johannes, about a month old, lay on the floor, whimpering lightly yet frightfully, just as he had fallen from the swaddling-table, while the wet-nurse stood staring stupidly.

The doctor, who tested the limbs of the contorted and jerking little body with firm, solicitous fingers, made a very, very serious face; the three girls stood sobbing in a corner and Frau Friedemann prayed aloud in the terror of her heart.

Even before the birth of the child the poor woman had been forced to undergo having her husband, the consul for the Netherlands, swept from her side by an illness as sudden as it was violent, and she was still too broken in spirit to be capable of hoping that little Johannes might be preserved to her. But after two days the physician, with an encouraging pressure of the hand, told her that an immediate danger was no longer to be feared; the slight concussion of the brain had, first of all, entirely disappeared, as one might see by the mere look of the eyes, which no longer had the same fixity as at the beginning. Of course, one would have to wait to know how, after all, the thing would develop — and, to be sure, to hope for the best, to hope for the best.

THE grey house with the gables in which Johannes Friedemann grew up stood near the northern gates of the old mercantile city, a city of medium size. Through the house door one entered a roomy vestibule, paved with stone tiles, from which a staircase with white-painted banister led to the upper stories. The wall-paper of the living-room in the first story revealed faded landscapes, and stiff-backed furniture stood ranged around the heavy mahogany table with the dark-red cover of plush.

Here he often sat during his childhood, at the window, in front of which beautiful flowers were always growing — sat on a little stool at the feet of his mother and listened to some wonderful story while he regarded the smooth, grey parting of her hair and her kind, gentle face and breathed the slight fragrance that always emanated from her. Or perhaps he would ask to see the picture of his father, a pleasant-looking gentleman with grey side-whiskers. He was in heaven, said his mother, and was awaiting them all there.

Behind the house there was a small garden, in which they spent a good part of the day during the summer, in spite of the sweetish vapours which were almost always being wafted across it from a neighbouring sugar-refinery. An old, gnarled walnut-tree grew there, and often little Johannes sat in its shade on a low wooden stool and cracked nuts, while Frau Friedemann and the three sisters, who were now grown up, sat together in a tent of grey canvas. The eyes of the mother often lifted themselves from her embroidery and wandered across to the child with pathetic tenderness.

He was not a beautiful child, little Johannes; and as he sat there on his stool with his pointed pigeon-breast, his hunched-up back, and his all too long, skinny arms, and cracked nuts with a great zest, he offered a most remarkable spectacle. His hands and feet, however, were small and delicate, and he had large, light-brown eyes, like those of a doe, a soft, well-cut mouth, and fine, light-brown hair. Although his head sat so lamentably between his shoulders, yet he was almost to be called beautiful.

WHEN he was seven years old, he was sent to school, and now the years went by swiftly and uniformly. Day by day, with that comically dignified manner of walking which is often a characteristic of the deformed, he would wander between the gabled houses and the shops to the old schoolhouse with the Gothic vaults; and when he had done his work at home, he would perhaps read in his books, with the lovely, coloured pictures on the covers, or occupy himself in the garden, while the sisters would tend house for the ailing mother. They also went to parties, for the Friedemanns belonged to the first families of the town; but the girls had unfortunately not yet married, for their fortune was not very large and they were rather plain-looking.

Johannes, to be sure, also received an invitation now and then from his companions of the same age, but he had no great pleasure in associating with them. He could not take part in their games, and as they al-

ways maintained a shy restraint towards him, com-
radeship was impossible.

There came the time when in the school-yard he
would often hear them talk of certain experiences;
he would listen with wide and attentive eyes as they
spoke of their ardour for this or that little girl, and
would remain silent. These things, which obviously
absorbed the others so completely, belonged to those
for which he was not suited, like gymnastics and ball-
throwing. Often this made him a bit sad; but, after all,
he had always been accustomed to stand by himself
and not to partake of the interests of the others.

In spite of this it happened — he was sixteen years
old at the time — that he conceived a sudden inclination for a girl of the same age. She was the sister of
one of his class-mates, a blond, wayward, merry creature, and he had become acquainted with her at her
brother's. He was seized by a strange awkwardness in
her presence, and the self-conscious and artificially
friendly manner with which she, too, treated him
filled him with deep sadness.

One summer afternoon as he was walking alone
upon the ramparts that lay beyond the town gates, he
heard a whispering behind a bush of jasmine and
peered cautiously between the branches. On the bench
which stood there sat that identical girl and beside her

207

a tall, red-haired boy whom he knew very well; he had his arm about her waist and was pressing upon her lips a kiss, which she returned, tittering. When Johannes Friedemann had seen this, he turned on his heels and went softly away.

His head sat deeper than ever between his shoulders, his hands trembled, and a sharp, insistent pain mounted from his breast into his throat. But he choked it down and carried himself resolutely erect, as well as he could. " Very well," he said to himself, " that is the end of that. I'll never again trouble myself about all this. It brings joy and happiness to others, but to me always only pain and sorrow. I am done with it. It is all over for me. Never again."

This resolution did him good. He renounced, renounced for ever. He went home and took up a book or played the violin, as he had learned to do in spite of his deformed breast.

When he was seventeen, he left school, in order to enter business life, as was the universal custom in that world of his. He obtained a position as an apprentice in the great lumber firm of Schlievogt and Company, down along the river. He was treated with consideration; he, on his part, was friendly and obliging; and so the time passed peacefully and all was in good order. In his twenty-first year his mother died after a long illness.

This was a great sorrow for Johannes Friedemann, a sorrow which he retained for a long time. He enjoyed this sorrow, he abandoned himself to it, just as one abandons oneself to a great happiness; he cultivated it with a thousand childhood memories and exploited it as his first deep experience.

Is not life in itself something good, whether or not it takes that form which one calls "happy"? Johannes Friedemann felt that and he loved life. No one can realize with what circumspection he, who had renounced the greatest happiness which life can offer us, knew how to enjoy the pleasures which lay open to him. A walk in springtime through the park that surrounded the town, the perfume of a flower, the song of a bird — might one not be thankful for such things?

And that a cultivated mind belongs to the capacity for enjoyment — yes, that a cultivated mind is always only the same thing as the capacity for enjoyment — that, too, he understood; and he cultivated himself. He loved music and went to all the concerts given in the town. Gradually he himself began to play the violin passably well, though he looked queer enough while playing, and he rejoiced in every soft and beautiful tone that he succeeded in producing. By constant reading he had also acquired a literary taste, which, no doubt, he shared with no one else in that town. He was well informed as to the latest books both at home and in foreign lands; he knew how to savour the rhythmic charm of a poem, knew how to let the intimate spirit of an exquisitely written short story work on him — oh! one might almost say that he was an epicurean.

He learned to comprehend that all things are worthy of enjoyment and that it is almost foolish to distinguish between happy and unhappy experiences. He accepted willingly all his feelings and moods and cultivated them, the sombre as well as the gay, and no less the wishes unfulfilled — his longings. He loved them for their own sakes and told himself that the best was lost through fulfilment. Is not the sweet, poignant, vague yearning and hoping of quiet evenings in spring more enjoyable than all the fulfilment which summer is able to bring? — Yes, he was an epicurean, was little Herr Friedemann!

Surely the people who greeted him on the streets in that compassionate, friendly manner to which he had become accustomed of old, did not know this. They did not know that this unfortunate cripple who marched through the streets full of droll dignity in his light-coloured overcoat and polished silk hat — he was, strangely enough, a bit vain — tenderly loved the life which flowed gently past him, void of great passion, but filled with a quiet and tender happiness which he knew how to create for himself.

THE chief hobby of Herr Friedemann, however, his actual passion, was the theatre. He possessed an uncommonly strong dramatic sensibility, and before powerful stage effects, or at the climax of a tragedy, his whole little body might begin to tremble. He had his special seat in the dress-circle of the municipal theatre, where he was to be seen regularly, and now and then his three sisters accompanied him. Since the death of their mother they kept house for him and themselves in the old home, which they owned in common.

Unluckily they were still not married; but they had long ago reached an age at which one becomes resigned, for Friederike, the oldest, was seventeen years older than Herr Friedemann. She and her sister Henriette were a trifle too tall and thin, while Pfiffi, the youngest, seemed far too short and stout. The last-named, moreover, had a droll trick of shaking herself at every word and then accumulating moisture in the corners of her mouth.

Little Herr Friedemann did not bother much about the three girls; but they kept faithfully together and were constantly of one mind. Especially when some engagement in their circle of acquaintances was announced, they would unanimously declare that this was really *most* delightful.

Their brother continued to live with them, even after he had left the timber firm of Schlievogt and Company and had gone into business by himself. He took over some small enterprise, an agency or the like, something that did not demand too much work. He used a few rooms on the ground-floor of the house, so that he only needed to climb the stairs to meals, for now and then he suffered a bit from asthma.

On his thirtieth birthday, a bright, warm June day, he sat in the grey garden-tent after lunch, with a new bolster, which Henriette had worked for him, behind his neck, a good cigar in his mouth, and a good book in his hand. Now and again he would put the book aside and listen to the joyous twittering of the sparrows which sat in the old nut-tree and gaze at the neat gravel-path that led to the house, and at the lawn, with the bright flower-beds.

Little Herr Friedemann did not wear a beard, and his face had practically not changed at all; only the

212

features had become a bit more pointed. His fine, light-brown hair he wore parted smoothly on the side.

Once as he let the book sink to his knees and blinked his eyes towards the blue, sunny heavens, he said to himself: " It's now thirty years. Now there will be perhaps another ten or even twenty. God knows. They will come quietly and silently and go by like those that are past, and I shall await them in tranquillity of soul."

In July of the same year that change in the post of commandant of the district took place which set that entire world agog. The portly, jovial gentleman who had occupied this post for long years had been a great favourite in social circles, and his departure was viewed with regret. God knows to what circumstance it was due that now Herr von Rinnlingen should have come here from the capital.

The exchange, moreover, did not seem to be a bad one, for the new Lieutenant-Colonel, who was married, but childless, rented a very roomy villa in the southern suburbs, and this led people to believe that he was planning receptions and the like. At all events the rumour that he was extraordinarily affluent was substantiated by the fact that he brought four

213

servants, five saddle- and carriage-horses, a landau, and a light trap with him.

This couple soon after their arrival began to pay calls on the most esteemed families, and their name was on all lips; but it was decidedly not Herr von Rinnlingen himself who aroused the most interest, but his wife. The men were staggered and for the present ventured no opinion, but the women were frank enough to show that they did not approve of the ways and nature of Gerda von Rinnlingen.

"It is natural that one should sense the air of the capital," asserted Frau Hagenström, the wife of the attorney, speaking to Henriette Friedemann, "quite natural. She smokes, she rides — no matter! But her conduct is not only free; it is loud, and even that is not the right word. You see, she is by no means ugly, one might even say that she was pretty; and yet she is quite devoid of feminine charm, and her look, her laugh, her movements, lack everything that men admire. She is not coquettish, and I, God knows, would be the last to disapprove of that; but is it right for such a young woman — she is twenty-four years old — to sacrifice completely all the natural, pretty powers of attraction? I am not very ready of speech, my dear, but I know what I mean. Our men are still, as it were, stunned. You will see that in a few weeks they will turn away from her completely disgusted."

"Well," said Fräulein Friedemann, " she is excellently provided for."

"Yes, her husband!" cried Frau Hagenström. "How does she treat him? You will see! I should be the first to insist that a married woman should to a certain degree be reserved towards the other sex. But how does she act towards her own husband? She has a way of giving him an ice-cold look and in a tone of pity saying: ' Dear friend ' to him, that arouses my indignation. For you ought to see *him* — correct, a fine figure of a man, courteous, a splendidly preserved man in the forties, a brilliant officer! They have been married four years, my dear."

THE spot in which little Herr Friedemann was to be vouchsafed to cast eyes upon Frau von Rinnlingen for the first time was the Hauptstrasse, which consisted almost exclusively of business houses, and this meeting took place at noon, just as he came from the Exchange, where he had joined in a conversation or two.

He was walking, tiny yet important, at the side of Herr Stephens, a wholesale merchant, an uncommonly large and bulky gentleman with round-trimmed side-whiskers and terribly thick eyebrows. Both wore top hats and because of the warm weather had opened their overcoats. They talked of politics, striking their walking-sticks rhythmically on the pavement; but when they had about reached the middle of the street, Herr Stephens, the wholesale merchant, suddenly said: "Devil take me, if there isn't the Von Rinnlingen driving towards us."

"Well met, now," said Herr Friedemann in his high, somewhat sharp voice and he looked expectantly straight ahead. "I have really not had a look at her yet. There we have the yellow wagon."

It was indeed the yellow hunting-trap, which Frau von Rinnlingen was using today, and she drove the two slender horses herself, while the footman, with crossed arms, sat behind her. She wore a wide jacket, very light in colour, and the skirt was also light. Her ruddy blond hair spread out from under the little round straw-hat with brown leather band, and was curled over her ears and fell in a thick knot on her neck. The colour of her oval face was a dull white, and in the corners of her brown eyes, which lay unusually close together, there were bluish shadows. Her short but well-shaped nose was saddled with freckles, which were very becoming to her; but one could not see whether her mouth was pretty or not, for she con-

216

stantly thrust out her under lip and then drew it back, rubbing it against the upper lip.

Stephens, the wholesale merchant, greeted her with extraordinary deference as the wagon reached them, and little Herr Friedemann also lifted his hat, looking at Frau von Rinnlingen with wide and attentive eyes. She lowered her whip, nodded her head slightly, and drove slowly past, looking to right and left at the houses and shop-windows.

After a few steps the wholesale merchant said: " She has been out driving and is now on the way home."

Little Herr Friedemann did not reply, but looked down at the pavement before him. Then suddenly he looked up at the wholesale merchant and asked: " What did you say? "

And Herr Stephens repeated his sagacious remark.

THREE days later at noon Johannes Friedemann returned home from his regular walk. Lunch took place at half past twelve and he was just about to go for half an hour to his " office," which was situated immediately to the right of the entrance door, when the servant-girl came across the entrance hall and said to him: " There are visitors here, Herr Friedemann."

" In the office? " he asked.

" No, upstairs, with the ladies."

" Who is it? "

" Lieutenant-Colonel and Frau von Rinnlingen."

" Oh," said Herr Friedemann, " then I will — "

And he ascended the stairs. On the second floor he walked across the hallway and he already had in his hand the knob of the lofty, white-painted door which opened into the " landscape room " when he suddenly halted, retreated a step, turned about, and went slowly back as he had come. And although he was completely alone, he said to himself, aloud: " No. Better not."

He went downstairs to his " office," sat down at the desk, and took up the newspaper. After a minute or so, however, he let it drop and looked sideways out of the window. He remained seated so until the girl came and told him that lunch was served; he then went up to the dining-room, where his sisters were already waiting for him, and sat down on his chair, on which three music-books were lying.

Henriette, who served the soup, said: " Johannes, guess who was here! "

" Well? " he asked.

" The new Lieutenant-Colonel and his wife."

" Really? Well, that was nice."

" Yes," said Pfiffi, and the corners of her mouth

began to water; " I find that they are both most agreeable persons."

" At all events," said Friederike, " we mustn't wait
too long with our return call. I suggest that we go the
day after tomorrow, Sunday."

" Sunday," said Henriette and Pfiffi.

" And, Johannes, you'll come with us, of course? "
asked Friederike.

" I should say so! " said Pfiffi and she shook herself. Herr Friedemann had utterly failed to hear the
question and ate his soup with a quiet and timorous
mien. It was as though he were listening to something,
to some strange sound.

On the following evening *Lohengrin* was on the boards
at the municipal theatre and all the best people were
present. The little auditorium was packed from top
to bottom and filled with buzzing noises, a smell
of gas, and perfumes. But all opera-glasses, in the
orchestra seats as well as those in the balconies, were
directed at box thirteen, just to the right of the stage,
for there for the first time Herr von Rinnlingen and
wife had made their appearance, and this was an opportunity, for once, to study the couple thoroughly.

When little Herr Friedemann, in an immacu-
late dress-suit, with a shining white shirt-bosom

projecting pointedly, entered his box —box thirteen — he started back, at the same time making a movement with his hand towards his forehead, while his nostrils expanded convulsively for a moment. But then he sat down on his chair, the seat to the left of Frau von Rinnlingen.

She looked at him a moment as he sat down, protruding her under lip, and then turned to exchange a few words with her husband, who stood behind her. He was a tall, broad-shouldered man with turned-up moustaches and a bronzed, good-natured face.

When the overture began and Frau von Rinnlingen leaned over the railing, Herr Friedemann shot a hasty side-glance at her. She wore a light-coloured evening dress and was even a trifle *décolleté* — the only one among the ladies present. Her sleeves were very wide and puffy, and her white gloves reached to her elbows. There was something voluptuous about her figure tonight, something that was not noticeable the other day, when she wore the wide jacket; her full bosom rose and sank slowly and the coils of ruddy-blond hair lay low and heavy upon her neck.

Herr Friedemann was pale, much paler than usual, and beneath his smoothly parted brown hair small beads of perspiration stood on his forehead. Frau von

220

Rinnlingen had stripped her glove from her left arm, which lay on the red velvet of the balustrade, and this round, dull-white arm, which like the unadorned hand was traversed by pale-blue veins, he saw always before him; there was no help for that.

The fiddles sang, the trumpets came in crashingly, Telramund fell, general jubilation reigned in the orchestra, and little Herr Friedemann sat immovably, pale and still, his head sunk deep between his shoulders, a forefinger pressed to his lips and his other hand under the lapel of his coat.

When the curtain fell, Frau von Rinnlingen rose and left the box with her husband. Herr Friedemann saw this without looking in that direction, passed his handkerchief lightly across his forehead, stood up suddenly, walked as far as the door leading to the corridor, turned back again, sat down in his place, and remained there motionless in the position which he had assumed before.

When the signal bell tinkled and his neighbours came back, he felt that Frau von Rinnlingen's eyes rested on him, and without really willing it he raised his head. As their glances met, she did not by any means look aside, but continued to regard him attentively without a trace of embarrassment, until he himself, conquered and humiliated, lowered his eyes. He

221

had grown still paler, and a strange, sweetish, biting anger began to rise in him. — The music began.

Towards the end of this act it happened that Frau von Rinnlingen let her fan slip from her hand and that this fell to the floor beside Herr Friedemann. Both bent down at the same time, but she seized it herself and said with a smile which had mockery in it: " I thank you."

Their heads had been close together and for a moment he had been forced to breathe the warm perfume of her breast. His face was distorted, his whole body contracted, and his heart pounded with such horribly heavy and powerful beats that his breath almost left him. He sat for another half-minute; then he pushed back his chair, stood up noiselessly, and noiselessly went out.

HE walked, followed by the strains of the music, across the corridor, received his silk hat, his light overcoat, and his cane at the coat-room, and strode down the steps to the street.

It was a warm, still evening. In the light of the gas lamps the grey, gabled houses stood silently against the heavens, which were glistening with bright, mild stars. The steps of the few people who passed Herr Friedemann echoed upon the pavement. Somebody greeted him, but he did not see it; he held his head low, and his high, pointed chest trembled, so heavily did he breathe. Now and then he said to himself softly: " My God! My God! "

He looked into his heart with horror-stricken and anxious eyes, and saw how his emotions, which he had cultivated so tenderly, had always treated so mildly and wisely, were now torn up, whirled about, twisted inside out. — And suddenly, quite overpowered, in a condition of dizziness, intoxication, longing, and torture, he leaned against a lamp-post and with trembling lips whispered: " Gerda! "

Everything remained quiet. Far and wide at this moment there was no human being to be seen. Little Herr Friedemann pulled himself together and walked on. He had gone along the street in which the theatre stood and which pitched rather steeply towards the river, and now he followed the Hauptstrasse towards the north, towards his home.

How she had looked at him! How? She had conquered him, forced him to lower his eyes? She had humiliated him with a look? Was she not a woman and he a man? And had not her remarkable brown eyes really trembled for joy during all this?

Once again he felt this impotent, almost voluptuous hatred rise within him, but then he thought of the

223

moment when her head had touched his own, when he had breathed the fragrance of her body, and he stood still for the second time, bent back his deformed chest and shoulders, drew his breath through his teeth, and then murmured once more, utterly bewildered, despairing, beyond himself: " My God! My God! "

And again he strode mechanically on, slowly, through the sultry evening air, through the empty, echoing streets, until he stood in front of his house. He stood still a moment in the hall and drew in the cool, cellar-like smell that prevailed there; then he entered his " office."

He sat down at the writing-desk by the open window and stared straight before him at a large, yellow rose, which someone had put there for him in a glass of water. He took it and breathed in its fragrance with closed eyes; but then with a weary and disconsolate gesture he pushed it aside. No, no, that was over! What was such fragrance to him now? What were all those things to him which up to the present had meant his " happiness "?

He turned aside and looked out at the quiet street. Now and again footsteps resounded and echoed past. The stars stood overhead and twinkled. How deathly tired and weak he had grown! His head seemed so empty and his despair began to dissolve into a great, gentle melancholy. A few lines of poetry swept through his memory, the music of *Lohengrin* rang again in his ears, once again he saw Frau von Rinnlingen's figure before him, her white arm upon the red velvet, and then he fell into a heavy, deep, feverish sleep.

HE was often close to waking, but he feared this and each time sank anew into unconsciousness. Then, after it had grown quite light, he opened his eyes and looked about him with large, sorrowful eyes. All things stood clear to his soul; it seemed as though his suffering had not been interrupted at all by sleep.

His head felt dull and his eyes burned; but after he had washed himself and wet his forehead with eau-de-Cologne, he felt better and sat down again quietly in his chair by the window, which had remained open. It was still very early in the morning, about five o'clock. Now and again a baker's boy went by; otherwise not a soul was to be seen. All the jalousies opposite were still down. But the birds were twittering and the sky was luminous and blue. It was a beautiful Sunday morning.

A feeling of comfort and confidence overcame little Herr Friedemann. Of what was he afraid? Were not all things as usual? Granted that he had had a bad attack yesterday; well, that was to be the end of it! It was not too late yet, he could still escape perdition! He must avoid every occasion that might renew the attack; he felt that he was strong enough for this. He felt that he had the strength to overcome it and to smother it wholly in his breast.

When the clock struck half past seven, Friederike entered and set the coffee-tray on the round table which stood in front of the leather sofa at the back of the room.

"Good-morning, Johannes," said she, "here is your breakfast."

"Thanks," said Herr Friedemann. And then: "Dear Friederike, I'm sorry that you will have to pay that call alone. I don't feel quite well enough to be able to go with you. I have slept badly, have a headache — in short, I must ask you — "

Friederike replied: "That is too bad. You can't entirely refrain from paying this call. But you really do look ill. Shall I lend you my menthol pencil?"

"Thanks," said Herr Friedemann. "It will pass." And Friederike went out.

Standing at the table, he drank his coffee slowly and ate a small *croissant*. He was satisfied with himself and proud of his determination. When he was done, he took a cigar and sat down once more at the

226

window. Breakfast had done him good and he felt happy and full of hope. He took up a book, read, smoked, and with blinking eyes looked out into the sunlight.

The street had now grown lively; a rattling of wagons, talk, and the tinkling of a horse-car sounded in his ears; but the twittering of birds was to be heard over all, and a warm, soft air was wafted from the gleaming blue sky.

At ten o'clock he heard the sisters crossing the hall, heard the entrance door creak, and saw the three ladies pass in front of the window, without paying any attention to it. An hour went by; he felt happier and happier.

A kind of excessive courage began to inspire him. What wonderful air, and how the birds twittered! How would it be if he took a short walk? — And then, suddenly, without any connecting idea, arose the sweet yet terrifying thought: " What if I went to her? " — And then, after he had suppressed by means of an actual muscular exertion all that arose in him of anxious warning, he added with a serene determination: " I'll go to her! "

And he donned his black Sunday suit, took his silk hat and cane, and walked quickly, and breathing hurriedly, through the entire town to the southern suburbs. Without looking at a single person, at every step he raised and lowered his head earnestly, utterly rapt in a state of forgetfulness and exaltation, until he stood in the chestnut avenue in front of the red villa at the entrance of which the name " Lieutenant-Colonel von Rinnlingen " was to be read.

HERE a trembling overcame him, and his heart beat hard and convulsively against his breast. But he entered the vestibule and rang the bell inside. The die was now cast and there was no going back. " Let all things take their course," he thought. Everything within him was now as still as death.

The door sprang open; the footman came towards him across the ante-room, took his card, and hastened up the stairs, on which lay a red carpet. Herr Friede-mann stared at this immovably until the servant came back and said the " *gnädige Frau* " begged him to come up.

Upstairs, close to the door of the drawing-room, where he left his cane, he cast a glance into the mirror. His face was pale, and above his reddened eyes his hair stuck to his forehead; the hand which held his silk hat trembled without his being able to stop it.

The servant opened the door and he entered. He found himself in a rather large, half-dark room; the

228

shades of the windows were drawn. To the right stood a grand piano, and in the centre, about the round table, were grouped arm-chairs upholstered in brown silk. Over the sofa, on the wall to the left, hung a landscape in a heavy gold frame. The wall-paper, too, was dark. Palms stood in a bay-window in the background.

A minute went by; then Frau von Rinnlingen drew aside the portieres to the right and came towards him soundlessly on the thick brown carpet. She wore a very simple red-and-black-checked dress. A shaft of sunlight fell into the room from the bay-window, and in this the motes danced. It caught her heavy reddish hair so that for a moment it gleamed like gold. She kept her remarkable eyes directed on him searchingly, and as usual thrust out her under lip.

" *Gnädige Frau,*" began Herr Friedemann, and looked up at her, for he reached only to her breast, " I too should like to pay you my respects. When you honoured my sisters with your call, I was, unfortunately, absent and — greatly regretted this — "

He really had nothing more to say, but she stood and looked at him remorselessly, as though she wished to force him to speak further. His blood rushed suddenly to his head. " She wishes to torture and mock me! " he thought, " and she sees through me! How her eyes quiver! "

229

Finally, in a very clear and very light voice, she said: " It is very kind of you to come. I too regretted not meeting you the other day. Will you please take a seat? "

She sat down close to him, laid her arms upon the arm-rests of the chair, and leaned back. He sat bent forward and held his hat between his knees.

She went on: " Do you know that your sisters were here a quarter of an hour ago? They told me you were ill."

" That is true," replied Herr Friedemann, " I didn't feel well this morning. I didn't think I should be able to go out. I beg you to excuse my being late."

" You don't appear in good health even now," she said very quietly, and looked him full in the face. " You are pale and your eyes are inflamed. Isn't your health generally good? "

" Oh — " stammered Herr Friedemann, " I am, in general, quite satisfied."

" I too am ill a good deal," she continued, without turning her eyes from him; " but nobody notices it. I am nervous and subject to the most remarkable conditions."

She ceased, inclined her chin upon her breast, and looked at him expectantly with upraised eyes. But he did not answer. He sat still and kept his eyes fixed upon her with a wide and thoughtful gaze. How strangely she spoke and how her light, uncontrolled voice moved him! His heart had grown quieter; it was as if he dreamed.

Frau von Rinnlingen began anew: " I am surely not mistaken — but didn't you leave the theatre yesterday before the close of the performance? "

" Yes, *gnädige Frau*."

" I was sorry for that. You were a most reverent neighbour, even though the performance was not good, or only relatively good. You love music? Do you play the piano? "

" I play the violin a little," said Herr Friedemann. " That is to say — it is almost none at all — "

" You play the violin? " she asked; then she looked abstractedly past him, and considered. Suddenly she said: " Why, we might play together now and then. I can accompany a bit. I should be glad to find some- one here — Would you come? "

" I should be glad to be of service to you," he re- plied, still as in a dream. A pause ensued. Then sud- denly the expression of her face changed. He saw how it became distorted with a scarcely perceptible expres- sion of pitiless mockery, how her eyes were again turned upon him, steadfastly and searchingly, as twice before, with that strange, mysterious quivering. His face grew fiery red; and without knowing where he should turn, completely flustered and beside himself, he let his head sink between his shoulders and looked down at the carpet, utterly lost. Like a short shudder that impotent, sweet, poignant fury went through him.

As he raised his eyes again with a desperate resolve, she refrained from looking at him, but directed her eyes over his head towards the door. Laboriously he brought forth a few words: " And are you at least in some way content with your sojourn in our city? "

" Oh," said Frau von Rinnlingen indifferently, " certainly. Why should I not be content? Of course I feel a bit narrowed here, a bit watched, but — Moreover," she went on rapidly, " before I forget it — we expect to have a few people here within the next few days, a small, informal company. We could make a bit of music, chat a bit — Then there is a very pretty garden behind the house; it extends down to the stream. In short, you and your ladies will, of course, receive an invitation, but I should like to ask you at once; will you give us the pleasure? "

Herr Friedemann had scarcely uttered his thanks and his acceptance when the door-handle was pressed down with energy and the Lieutenant-Colonel entered. Both rose, and while Frau von Rinnlingen introduced the gentlemen to each other, her husband bowed to Herr Friedemann and to her with equal courtesy. His brown face was quite suffused with warmth.

While drawing off his gloves, he said something to Herr Friedemann in his strong and incisive voice and Herr Friedemann looked up at him with his large, expressionless eyes and half expected to be kindlily patted on the shoulder. Then with heels drawn together and the upper part of his body slightly bent forward the Lieutenant-Colonel turned to his wife and said, with perceptibly softened voice: " Have you asked Herr Friedemann for the pleasure of his company at our little reception, my dear? If it is agreeable to you, I think we might have it in about a week. I hope that the weather will continue good and that we can make use of the garden."

" As you think best," said Frau von Rinnlingen and looked straight past him.

Two minutes later Herr Friedemann bade them good-bye. As he bowed once more at the threshold, he met their eyes, which rested upon him without any expression.

HE went away, but not back to town; involuntarily he chose a way which branched off from the avenue and led to the former ramparts along the river. There were well-tended lawns there, shady paths, and benches.

He walked quickly and unconsciously, without looking up. He was unbearably hot, and he felt the fires within him rise and fall, and a merciless throbbing in his weary head.

Were not her eyes still resting upon him? Not as when he left, however, empty and void of expression, but as before, with that trembling cruelty, as when she had spoken to him in that strange, quiet manner? Oh, did it delight her to render him helpless and to put him beside himself? Even though she saw through him, might she not have a bit of pity for him?

He had walked below, along the river, close to the green grass-covered bastions, and he sat down on a bench which was surrounded by jasmine-bushes in a half-circle. Everything about him was full of a sweet, sultry fragrance. In front of him the sun brooded upon the trembling water.

How tired and exhausted he felt, and yet how all things were in tortured revolt within him! Would it not be best to look about him once more and then go down into the still water, after a brief pang to be freed, rescued unto a deep rest? Ah, rest, rest it was that he yearned for! Not rest within a void and un-

234

hearing nothingness, however, but a peace lighted by a soft and gentle sun, filled by sweet, quiet thoughts.

His entire tender love of life thrilled through him at this moment, and a deep longing for his lost happiness. But then he looked about him into the silent, eternal, indifferent peace of nature, saw how the river pursued its course in the sun, how the grass moved tremblingly and the flowers stood where they had blossomed, in order then to wither and decay, saw how all things, all things, were bound to destiny with this dumb surrender — and then suddenly he was overcome by a feeling of friendliness and acquiescence in the necessity which was able to give man a kind of superiority over all fate.

He thought of that afternoon on his thirtieth birthday, when, happy in the possession of content, he had believed he was able to survey the rest of his life without fear or hope. He had seen neither light nor shadow then, but everything had lain before him in a mild twilight, until far below him it merged, almost imperceptibly, into the dark, and he had contemplated the years that were still to come with a quiet and superior smile — how long ago was that?

And then this woman had come, she was bound to come, it was his fate, she herself was his fate, she alone! Had he not felt this from the very first moment? She had come, and though he had striven to defend his peace — all the forces within him were bound to rise in revolt for her, all that from youth onward he had suppressed in himself because he felt that it would mean ruin and torment to him — this had seized him with a terrible, irresistible power and was bringing him to ruin!

It was bringing him to ruin — he felt that. But why struggle and torture himself? Let everything take its course! He would go his way and close his eyes to the yawning abyss behind there, obedient to fate, obedient to the puissant, poignant, sweet power that no one could elude.

The water glistened, the jasmine breathed forth its keen, sultry fragrance, the birds twittered everywhere about him in the trees, between which shone a heavy, velvety blue sky. But little hunch-backed Herr Friedemann continued to sit for a long time upon his bench. He sat bending forward, his forehead propped in both hands.

ALL were agreed that this affair at Rinnlingen's was most enjoyable. Some thirty persons sat at the long, tastefully decorated table which extended through the wide dining-room; the footman and two servants were already hurrying about with the ices; there was a clinking, a clattering, and a warm odour of food and perfume. Affable wholesale merchants with their wives and daughters were assembled here; in addition almost all the officers of the garrison, an old, beloved physician, a few lawyers, and such others as belonged to the best circles. A student of mathematics was also present, a nephew of the Lieutenant-Colonel, who was on a visit to his relations; he carried on the most abstruse conversations with Fräulein Hagenström, who sat opposite Herr Friedemann.

He himself sat on a beautiful velvet cushion at the lower end of the table, next to the unbeautiful wife of the headmaster of the school, not far from Frau von Rinnlingen, who had been escorted to the table by Consul Stephens. It was surprising what a change had taken place in little Herr Friedemann during the last week. It was, perhaps, the fault of the whitish incandescent gas-light which flooded the room that his face appeared so terribly pale; but his cheeks had sunken in, his eyes, reddened and surrounded by dark shadows, revealed an unutterably sad glimmer, and it seemed as though his figure was more deformed than ever. — He drank a good deal of wine and now and then spoke a few words to his table-companion.

Frau von Rinnlingen had as yet exchanged not a single word with Herr Friedemann at table; now she bent forward a little and called to him: "I waited for you in vain these days, for you and your fiddle."

He looked at her a moment in complete absence of mind before he answered. She wore a light-coloured, airy costume which exposed her white throat, and a Maréchal Niel rose in full flower was fastened in her bright hair. Her cheeks this evening were a trifle flushed, but as usual blue shadows lay in the corners of her eyes.

Herr Friedemann looked down on his plate and produced some kind of answer, whereupon he was obliged to reply to a question of the headmaster's wife, whether he loved Beethoven. At this moment, however, the Lieutenant-Colonel, who sat at the upper end of the table, caught his wife's eye, tapped on his glass, and said: "Ladies and gentlemen, I suggest that we take our coffee in the other rooms; and then the garden tonight must be not at all bad, and if anyone wishes to draw a breath of fresh air there, I am with him."

In the silence which ensued Lieutenant von Deidesheim tactfully made a witty remark, so that everybody rose amid merry laughter. Herr Friedemann was one of the last to leave the room with his lady; he led her through the Old German room, in which the men were beginning to smoke, into the half-dark and comfortable living-room, and left her.

He was dressed with great care; his coat was fault-less, his shirt immaculately white; and his small and well-shaped feet were covered by patent-leather shoes. Now and then one could see that he wore red silk socks.

He looked out into the corridor and saw that larger groups were already going down the steps into the garden. But he sat down with his cigar and his coffee near the door of the Old German room, in which several gentlemen stood chatting together, and looked into the living-room.

Immediately to the right of the door a group sat about a small table, the centre of which was the student, who spoke with enthusiasm. He had made the assertion that more than one parallel to a straight line could be drawn through a point; Frau Hagenström, the wife of the attorney-at-law, had exclaimed: " That's impossible! " and now it was strikingly manifest that all pretended to have understood it.

But in the back of the room, on the ottoman, close to the low, red-shaded lamp, sat Gerda von Rinnlingen in conversation with young Fräulein Stephens. She sat leaning back a little on the yellow silk cushions, one foot placed over the other, and slowly smoked a

239

cigarette, exhaling the smoke through the nose and thrusting forward her under lip. Fräulein Stephens sat upright and as though carved from wood and made her replies, smiling anxiously.

No one paid any attention to little Herr Friedemann, and no one observed that his big eyes were unremittingly directed upon Frau von Rinnlingen. He sat in a relaxed position and regarded her. There was nothing like passion in his look, and hardly any pain; something dull and dead lay in it, a heavy, powerless, and will-less surrender.

Ten minutes or so went by in this way; then Frau von Rinnlingen rose suddenly, and without looking at him, as though she had secretly observed him during the entire time, she went up to him and remained standing before him. He stood up, lifted his eyes to her, and heard the words: " Should you care to accompany me into the garden, Herr Friedemann? "

He replied: " With pleasure, *gnädige Frau.*"

" You haven't yet seen our garden? " she asked, as they stood on the steps. " It is pretty large. I hope that there won't be too many people there yet; I should like to draw a bit of fresh air. I got a headache during the dinner; possibly this claret was too strong for me. — Here, we must go out through this door." It was a glass door, which opened from the ante-room on a small, cool lobby; then a few steps led to the open air.

In the wonderful, warm, star-bright night, fragrance streamed from every flower-bed. The garden lay in full moonlight, and the guests walked up and down the white luminous gravel-paths, chatting and smoking. A group had assembled about the fountain, where the old, beloved physician amid general laughter was setting paper boats afloat.

Frau von Rinnlingen passed by with a slight inclination of her head, and pointed to the distance, where the pretty and fragrant flower-garden darkened to the denseness of a park.

" We will go down the central path," she said. Two low, broad obelisks stood at the entrance.

Behind there, at the end of the straight avenue of chestnuts, they saw the river gleaming blank and green in the moonlight. Everything about was dark and cool. Here and there a side path branched off, which no doubt also curved towards the river. For a long time no sound was heard.

" Close to the water," she said, " is a pretty place, where I have often sat. There we can chat for a moment. — Just see, now and again a star glitters through the leafage."

He did not answer, but looked at the green,

shimmering surface which they were nearing. One could see the opposite bank, the park about the ramparts. As they left the avenue and stepped out on the lawn which inclined towards the river, Frau von Rinnlingen remarked: " Here is our place, a little to the right; see, it's unoccupied."

The bench on which they sat down stood close to the park, six steps to the side of the avenue. It was warmer here than between the broad trees. The crickets chirped in the grass, which close to the water passed into thin reeds. The moon-bright river reflected a mild light.

Both were silent for a while and looked at the water. Then, completely shaken, he heard the very voice he had heard a week before; this soft, deliberate, and tender tone moved him again.

" Since when have you had your affliction, Herr Friedemann? " she asked. " Were you born with it? "

He swallowed hard, for his throat was as if he were strangling. Then he replied, softly and politely: " No, *gnädige Frau*, I was dropped on the floor as a little child; it comes from that."

" And how old are you now? " she went on.

" Thirty years, *gnädige Frau*."

" Thirty years," she repeated. " And you have not been happy, these thirty years? "

242

Herr Friedemann shook his head, and his lips quivered. " No," said he; " that was falsehood and imagination."

" So you believed you were happy? " she asked.

" I tried to," he said, and she replied:

" That was brave."

A minute went by. Only the crickets chirped, and behind them the trees rustled very softly.

" I understand a little about unhappiness," she then said. " Such summer nights along the water are the best thing for it."

He did not reply to this, but pointed with a feeble gesture to the other bank, which lay peacefully in the dark.

" I sat there the other day," he said.

" After you left me? " she asked.

He merely nodded.

Then suddenly he sprang up from his seat, sobbed, gave vent to a cry, a cry of complaint which at the same time had something liberating in it, and sank slowly to the ground at her feet. He had touched her hand with his, as it rested on the bench beside him, and while he held it fast, while he seized the other also, while this quite deformed little man lay twitching and quivering upon his knees before her and buried his face in her lap, he stammered in a hoarse, inhuman voice: " You know it — let me — I can't go on — my God — my God — "

She did not resist him, nor did she bend down to him. She sat fully erect, leaning a little away from him, and her small eyes, which lay so close together and in which the damp shimmer of the water seemed to mirror itself, stared fixedly straight in front of her, over his head, into the distance.

And then suddenly, with a jerk, with a short, proud, contemptuous laugh, she had torn her hands from his hot fingers, had seized his arm, thrown him sideways flat upon the ground, sprung up, and vanished in the avenue.

He lay there, his face in the grass, stunned, beside himself; and every moment a quiver went through his body. He drew himself together, made two steps, and fell to the ground once more. He lay close to the water.

What actually went on in him during what followed now? Perhaps it was that voluptuous hate which he had felt when she humiliated him by her look, a hate which now, as he lay on the ground, after being treated by her like a dog, resolved itself into an insane fury, which called for action, even though it should be against himself — perhaps disgust at himself, which filled him with a thirst to destroy himself, to tear himself to pieces, to extinguish himself.

He pushed himself still further forward upon his stomach, lifted the upper part of his body, and let it fall into the water. He did not lift his head again; he did not once move his legs, which lay on the bank.

At the splashing of the water the crickets had for a moment grown silent. Now their chirping began again, the park rustled softly, and down through the long avenue came subdued laughter.

1897

THE WARDROBE

THE WARDROBE

It was cloudy, dusky, and cool when the Berlin-Rome express entered a railway station of medium size. In a first-class compartment, with lace covers over the backs of the broad plush seats, a lone traveller straightened himself up: Albrecht van der Qualen. He awoke. He experienced a sickly taste in his mouth, and his body was full of that not very agreeable feeling which is evoked by a standstill after a long journey, the silencing of the rhythmic rolling thud, the stillness which affords such a marked contrast to the noises without, the calls and signals. — This condition is like coming to out of a state of intoxication, of insensibility. Our nerves are suddenly deprived of the support, the rhythm, to which they had surrendered; now they feel themselves utterly disturbed and abandoned. And this is all the more pronounced when simultaneously we awake out of the dull sleep of a railway journey.

Albrecht van der Qualen stretched himself a bit, stepped to the window, and let down the sash. He glanced along the length of the train. At the forward end a number of men were busy loading and unloading parcels. The locomotive gave vent to more noises, sneezed and growled a little, and then became still and silent, but only as a horse stands still, lifting its hoof, twitching its ears, and waiting eagerly for the signal to start. A large, stout lady in a long rain-coat perseveringly dragged a travelling-bag which must have weighed a hundredweight to and fro alongside the train, shoving it ahead of her by jerks of one knee. Her face was infinitely care-worn; she was dumb, hounded, with anxious eyes. Especially her upper lip, which she protruded considerably and which was beaded with tiny drops of sweat, had something unutterably pathetic about it. " You poor, dear creature! " thought Van der Qualen. " If I could help you, give you shelter, comfort you, only for the sake of that upper lip of yours! But everyone for himself, that's the way life is arranged, and I, who am at this moment quite free from anxiety, am standing here and looking at you as though you were a beetle that had fallen on its back."

Twilight reigned in the modest railway station. Was it evening or morning? He did not know. He had slept, and it was absolutely impossible to say whether he had slept for two, five, or twelve hours. Had he not even upon occasion slept for twenty-four hours and longer, without the slightest interruption — a deep, an extraordinarily deep sleep? — He was a gentleman in a dark-brown winter overcoat of half length, with a velvet collar. It was very difficult to tell his age from his features; one might have hesitated between twenty-five and the close of the thirties. His complexion was yellow, but his eyes were of a glowing black, like coals, and surrounded by deep shadows. These eyes boded no good. Various physicians, in frank and serious conversations with him, had given him only a few months more to live. — His hair, by the way, was dark and parted smoothly on the side.

In Berlin — though Berlin was not the starting-point of his journey — by chance he had boarded the departing express with his red hand-bag; he had slept, and now, having awakened, he felt himself so completely freed from all sense of time that a feeling of comfort permeated him. He owned no watch. He was happy in the thought that the thin chain of gold that he wore round his neck bore only a small medallion, which he carried in his waistcoat-pocket. He did not care to know what hour it was, nor even what day of the week, for he also refrained from using a calendar. For some time past he had rid himself of the habit of knowing the day of the month or even the

251

month itself — yes, even the particular year. All
things must float in the air, he was used to think, and
he considered this to mean a great deal, though it was
a pretty murky turn of phrase. Seldom or never was
he disturbed in this ignorance, since he did his utmost
to keep all such disturbances at a distance. Surely it
was enough to know approximately what season it
happened to be? "It is approximately autumn," he
thought as he looked out into the dusky and damp station. "I know no more than that! Have I the least idea
where I am?"

And suddenly this thought reduced the satisfaction
that he felt to a kind of joyous horror. No, he did not
know where he was! Was he still in Germany? No
doubt. In North Germany? That remained to be seen!
His eyes, still stupid from sleep, had seen a lighted
sign glide past the window of his compartment, and
this sign had possibly displayed the name of the station — no image of a single letter had penetrated to
his brain. Still in his state of stupor he had heard the
conductor call out the name two or three times — not
a single syllable had he caught. But there, there, in a
twilight of which he did not know whether it meant
morning or evening, lay a strange place, an unknown
city. — Albrecht van der Qualen took his felt hat out
of the net and seized his red leather travelling-bag,

the strap of which clasped at the same time a red and white checked travelling-rug of silk and wool, in which, again, was stuck an umbrella with a silver handle. And although his ticket was booked to Florence, he left the compartment, strode through the modest station, put his baggage in the cloak-room, lighted a cigar, thrust his hands — he carried neither stick nor umbrella — into the pockets of his overcoat, and left the station.

Outside, in the dusky, damp, and rather empty square five or six coachmen cracked their whips, and a man with a gold-braided cap and a long cape, which he shiveringly wrapped about himself, said with questioning accent: " The Honest Man Inn? " Van der Qualen thanked him courteously and walked straight ahead. The people whom he met had turned up the collars of their coats; for this reason he did so too, nestled his chin against the velvet, puffed at his cigar, and strode on, not fast and not slowly.

He passed a low wall and an old stone gate with two massive towers, and crossed a bridge, on the ramparts of which stood statues; the water rolled beneath, turbidly and lazily. A long, half-rotten barge came by; in the stern a man was steering with a long pole. Van der Qualen stood still for a while and leaned over the wall of the bridge. " Just see," he thought, " a

253

river; the river. It is well that I don't know its ordinary name." — And then he went on.

He continued to walk a little longer upon the pavement of a street which was neither very broad nor very narrow, and then struck off somewhere to the left. It was evening. The electric arc-lamps flared up, sputtered a few times, glowed, hissed, and then lighted up the fog. The shops closed. " Very well," thought Van der Qualen, " let us say that it is in every respect autumn," and he strode along on the dark wet pavement. He wore no galoshes, but his boots were extraordinarily broad, solid, and durable, though by no means lacking in elegance.

He walked continuously towards the left. People strode and hurried past him, went about their business or came from their business. " And here I am walking right among them," he thought, " and am more alone and strange than apparently any other human being has ever been. I have no business and no goal. I have not even a walking-stick for a support. No one could be less attached, freer, less interested. No one owes anything to me; I owe no one anything. God has never extended His hand over me; He does not know me at all. A good faithful misfortune without alms is a good thing; one may then say to oneself: ' I owe nothing to God.' "

The city soon came to an end. Most likely he had proceeded from the centre towards the periphery. He found himself upon a broad suburban street with trees and villas, bent towards the right, passed three or four almost rustic streets, lighted only by gas-lamps, and finally stood still in one that was a little wider, in front of a wooden gate. This was to the right of an ordinary house, painted a turbid yellow, a house distinguished only by utterly untransparent and boldly curved plate-glass windows. There was a plate attached to the gate, with the inscription: " Rooms to let — third story." " Really? " said he; he threw away the stump of his cigar, passed through the gate, along a plank which divided this piece of land from the neighbouring one, then to the left through the entrance door, and across the vestibule, which was covered by a cheap strip of carpet, a kind of old grey cover, and began to mount the humble wooden stairs.

The doors to the flats were also very modest, with panes of frosted glass, protected by wire-cloth, and each bore some kind of name-plate. The landings of the staircase were lighted by oil-lamps. In the third story, however — it was the topmost, and after that came the attic — there were also entrances to right and left of the staircase — simple brownish doors; no name was to be seen. Van der Qualen pulled the brass bell-knob in the middle. — The bell rang, but no movement was heard from within. He knocked at the door to the left. — No answer. He knocked at the door to the right. — Light, slow footsteps were heard and the door opened.

It was a woman, a large, lean dame, old and tall. She wore a cap with a large bow of dull lilac, and an old-fashioned, faded black dress. She revealed an emaciated, birdlike face, and upon her forehead a patch of eruptions was visible, a mosslike growth. It was a rather revolting thing.

" Good-evening," said Van der Qualen. " The rooms — "

The old lady nodded; she nodded and smiled slowly, dumb and full of understanding, and pointed with a beautiful, white, slender hand, with a slow, tired, and aristocratic gesture towards the opposite door, that to the left. She then withdrew and soon reappeared with a key. " Just see," thought Van der Qualen, who stood behind her, while she unlocked the door. " You are like a nightmare, like a figure out of the tales of Hoffmann, my gracious lady." — She took the oil-lamp from the bracket and bade him enter.

It was a small low-ceiled room with a brown floor;

the walls, however, were covered with straw-coloured mats up to the top. The window in the rear wall to the right was hidden by the long, slender folds of a white muslin curtain. The white door to the adjoining room was on the right hand.

The old lady opened this door and held up the lamp. This room was miserably bare, with naked, white walls, against which three wicker chairs, enamelled bright red, stood relieved like strawberries against whipped cream. A wardrobe, a wash-stand and mirror — The bed, an extraordinarily huge piece of mahogany furniture, stood free in the middle of the room.

" Have you any objection to it? " asked the old lady, and she passed her beautiful, slender white hand lightly across the mosslike growth on her forehead. — It seemed as though she said this merely casually, as though she could not think of anything more commonplace to say for the moment. She at once added: " So to speak — ? "

" No, I have no objection to it," said Van der Qualen. " The rooms are fitted out rather — well, cleverly. I'll take them. — I should like someone to fetch my things from the railway station — here is the check. Please see to it that the bed and the night-table are put in order — and let me have the front door key,

257

as well as the key to the flat — and also a couple of towels. I should like to wash and dress a bit, then go and dine in the city and return later on."

He drew a nickel-plated case from his pocket, took out a piece of soap, and began to wash his face and hands at the wash-stand. Meantime he peered through window-panes which curved markedly outward, far down over the muddy suburban streets in the gas-light, on arc-lamps and villas. — Drying his hands, he crossed to the wardrobe. It was a four-square, brown-stained thing, a little wobbly, with an absurdly ornate top, and stood in the middle of the right wall, exactly in the niche of a second white door, which must lead to the rooms to which the entrance was through the main and middle doors out on the landing. " A few things in this world are well arranged," thought Van der Qualen. " This wardrobe fits into the niche of the door as though it had been made for it." — He opened it. — The wardrobe was completely empty, with several rows of hooks in the upper part; but it was evident that this solid piece of furniture had no back whatever; it was shut off behind by a grey stuff, hard, common canvas, which was fastened to the four corners by nails or drawing-pins.

Van der Qualen closed the wardrobe, took up his hat, turned up the collar of his overcoat again, extinguished the candle, and went forth. As he passed through the front room, he thought he heard, between the sounds of his footsteps, in the adjoining rooms, a tinkling noise, a light, clear metallic tone — but it was altogether unsafe to say whether this was not an illusion. " It is as though a golden ring fell into a silver basin," thought he, as he locked the door to the flat, descended the stairs, left the house, and found his way back to the city.

He entered a well-lighted restaurant in a lively street and sat down at one of the front tables, turning his back to everybody. He ate a vegetable soup with toasted bread, a beefsteak with an egg, stewed fruit, and wine, a bit of green Gorgonzola, and half a pear. As he paid and put on his overcoat, he gave a few puffs at a Russian cigarette, then lighted a cigar, and went out. He strolled about a bit, found his way to his suburb, and retraced it without haste.

The house with the plate-glass windows stood there wholly dark and silent, as Van der Qualen opened the house door and mounted the dark stairs. He lighted his way up with a match, and, at the third story, opened the brown door to the left which led to his room. After he had laid his overcoat and hat on the sofa, he lighted the lamp on the big desk and found there his travelling-bag, as well as the plaid rug and the umbrella. He unrolled the rug and drew forth a flask of brandy, took a small glass out of his bag, and, while he sat in an arm-chair and smoked his cigar to a finish, took a sip from time to time. " It's pleasant," he thought, " that there is still brandy to be had in the world." — He then went into the bedroom, where he lighted the candle on the night-table, put out the lamp in the other room, and began to undress. He laid his grey, inconspicuous, and durable suit, piece by piece, on the red chair beside the bed; then, however, as he loosened his braces, he remembered his hat and over-coat, which still lay on the sofa; he fetched them, he opened the wardrobe — He made a step backwards and felt behind him for one of the large, dark-red mahogany balls which decorated the four corners of the bed.

The room with its bare, white walls, against which the red-lacquered chairs stood relieved like strawberries against whipped cream, stood revealed in the unsteady light of the candle. But there, the wardrobe, the door of which stood wide open, was not empty; some-one stood within it, a figure, a creature, so lovely that Albrecht van der Qualen's heart stood still for a moment and then resumed its beating with full, slow, gentle throbs. — She was quite naked and held up one of her small, delicate arms, for she was clutching one

of the hooks in the top of the wardrobe with her forefinger. Ripples of her long, brown hair rested upon
her childlike shoulders, which breathed forth a beauty
which could be answered only by sobs. Her long, black
eyes mirrored the light of the candle. — Her mouth
was a trifle wide, but its expression was as sweet as
the lips of sleep when they touch our forehead after
days of suffering. She kept her heels close together,
and her slender legs caressed each other.

Albrecht van der Qualen passed his hand across
his eyes and saw — he saw that the grey canvas had
been unloosened from the right corner of the wardrobe.

"How—" said he. "Won't you come in?—or
what should I say — come out? May I offer you a
glass of brandy? Half a glass? . . ." But he expected
no answer to these questions, and received none. Her
small, shining eyes, so black that they appeared to be
without expression, unfathomable and dumb — they
were directed upon him, but without fixity or aim,
vague, and as though they did not see him.

"Shall I tell you a story?" she suddenly asked in a
quiet, veiled voice.

"Tell it," he replied. He had sunk in a sitting position on the edge of the bed, the overcoat rested
upon his knees, and his folded hands lay upon it.

261

His mouth stood a trifle open, and his eyes were half closed. But his blood pulsed warmly and mildly through his body, and there was a soft humming in his ears.

She had sunk down in the wardrobe and had clasped with her delicate arms one of her knees, which she had drawn up, while the other leg dangled outside. Her small breasts were pressed together by the upper part of her arms, and the taut skin of her knee shone. She told her story — told it in a soft voice, while the candle flame executed silent dances.

" A couple were walking across the heath, and her head lay upon his shoulder. The herbs sent forth a strong scent, but the cloudy mists of evening were already rising from the ground." Thus it began. And sometimes there were verses, which rhymed in so incomparably light and sweet a way that we are able to achieve it only now and then during nights of fever in a half-sleep. But the thing did not come to a good close. The end was as sad as when two hold each other in an inextricable embrace, and while their lips are pressed together, one of them thrusts a broad knife into the body of the other, just above the belt, and for good reasons. But that was the way it ended. And then, with a gesture of infinite quiet modesty, she lifted the right-hand corner of the grey stuff which constituted the back wall of the wardrobe, and was no longer there.

FROM now on he found her in his wardrobe every night and listened to her. — How many evenings? How many days, weeks, or months did he remain in this dwelling and in this city? — It would do no one any good if the number were put down here. Who would take any joy in a paltry figure? — And we know that several doctors had granted Albrecht van der Qualen only a few months more.

She told him stories. And they were melancholy stories, void of comfort; but they sank like a sweet burden upon his heart and let it beat more slowly and happily. Often he forgot himself. — His blood rebelled within him, he stretched out his hands to her, and she did not resist him. But then he would not find her in the wardrobe for several nights, and when she returned, she would tell no stories for several more nights, and then slowly began again, until he forgot himself once more.

How long did this last — who knows? Who knows, moreover, whether Albrecht van der Qualen really awakened that afternoon and betook himself to the unknown city; whether he did not rather remain sleeping in his first-class compartment, to be borne by the

Berlin-Rome express with tremendous speed across the mountains? Who among us would presume to give a definite answer to this question, upon his own responsibility? That is quite uncertain. " All things must float in the air — "

1899

COM